Easy Sunday

Cities

www.barbarianspy.com

WARNING: This book is for sale to **ADULT AUDIENCES ONLY**. Contains graphic gay male sex, multiple partners, anal sex, interracial sex, and gay love all of which may be considered offensive by some readers.

All sexually active characters in this work are at least 18 years of age.

BarbarianSpy
Toronto, Australia

Easy Sunday

Cities

A Day to Cut Loose

Habu

Table of Contents

Chapter One: New York Sunday

"I don't believe I've seen you walking the runway at one of these shows before."

Gene Worth looked over at the man adjusting something on the standing frame of the floodlight as the last of the gawkers were clearing out of the Studio D room of Punto on New York's West 38th Street. There was nothing not to like about the guy, who was maybe in his late thirties, Hispanic, muscular, easy on the eyes, attentive to his business, and full of self-confidence. Gene couldn't help to have seen that the guy had been attentive to him as well as he walked the long, raised platform strip down the center of the room in the House of Havlos young men's fashions show. He'd been particularly attentive when Gene was modeling a "barely there" swimsuit with sandals and a pool jacket he'd slipped off half way down the room and flipped casually over his shoulder.

"No, you haven't. This was my first gig here," Gene answered.

"Manny Rodriguez, here," the Hispanic muscleman said holding his hand out and flashing Gene a smile. "Manny's New Yorkese for Manuel. If you do more shows—and I'm sure you will, because you were a knockout in this one—you'll see me around a lot." Gene took the hand. He couldn't very well not do so without being impolite, and he had had the urge to touch the man from the time they'd first locked eyes anyway. It was Sunday, his "easy" day. And the fashion show had put him in heat. The gawkers had been very close to the walkers all the way down the long aisle and Gene had caught many a look from a Class A looker—both female and male—that undressed him and messed with him. He couldn't help but feel stroked sexually by that. There was no doubt he'd do more runway work if he could get it.

And it was Sunday.

Manny held his hand for a few beats longer than necessary and folded a thumb under between their palms and stroked Gene's palm with it a few times before letting the hand go. Gene recognized the universal signal between gay men. Gene wasn't exactly gay; he went with both women and men, but he'd gone with enough men to recognize and appreciate the signal. The signal not only announced "gay," but since Manny had taken the initiative, it announced "top" as well—top in search of a bottom.

Gene looked into Manny's eyes and smiled. He dipped his head slightly, and he heard Manny take his breath in. The smile was a "me too" on being gay, and the head dip was a signal of submission—putting the two together as he had done meant "I'm available and I'm available to you." Just like that, the playing field had been established.

"I didn't get lunch because of the setup required for the show," Manny said, looking directly at Gene and signaling that it wasn't just lunch he was talking about. "I think I saw you here early too. Interested in going to get something to eat with me? My treat."

"Why not, it's Sunday," Gene answered.

Manny gave him a quizzical look, but he didn't ask. He was getting what he wanted. The cute little piece was going to go with him and Manny was going to fuck him. The gorgeous little male model was being easy—far easier than Manny had anticipated he would be.

"And then maybe—" he started to say.

"Sure, why not, it's Sunday," Gene said again. This was met with another quizzical look from Manny but the cutie was saying yes to everything he suggested so far, so he wasn't going to get into an analysis of what was running smoothly.

Manny had said he knew where there was a cheap café nearby that served reasonably good food, if that was OK with Gene. "I don't live far from here," he said, looking pointedly at Gene. "But I don't want to come across as cheap or anything, if you're used to something fancier than burgers."

"I'm not used to fancy, no. I'm a student and on my own."

"Not high school, I hope," Manny said with the hint of a nervous laugh. He flashed that meaningful "just checking" look again.

"No. I'm finishing up college—a year early—and am starting in a graduate program. I'm twenty-one."

"Good. I mean it's good that you're getting an education. I didn't have the interest to go beyond high school, but I've sure learned the lighting business the 'just do it' way."

"Yeah, I watch you. I could tell you knew what you were doing."

"I know what I'm doing about a lot of things," Manny said with a slight smile. He checked Gene's face to see if the double entendre had struck home and saw that it had. God, he wondered, how could a guy this good looking be this easy.

They had walked as they talked and it wasn't long before they were seated in the café. Gene indeed seemed satisfied with the food and he didn't balk either at Manny's being expressive with his hands, touching Gene on the forearm and shoulder and knee and thigh as they talked. Gene racked it up to hot Latin blood. The hot Latin he was eating with heated him up too. Manny knew, though, it was because he could hardly contain his need to fuck the gorgeous young man.

"You say this was your first modeling gig and you're finishing up college?" Manny said. He obviously was digging for more information. "A college here in New York? And how did you get signed up for modeling? You walked the catwalk like a seasoned pro." That modeling style had been what had made Manny think this hunt was going to be difficult. Gene had the "ice maiden/I'm just an automated dressing mannequin" look professional models maintain on the runway down pat.

"They trained me for that in college," Gene said. "I'm up from Philadelphia just for the weekend, but I'll have to move here. I've got a job signed up with this fashion house if I did well enough today—"

"You did great today," Manny interjected.

"Thanks," Gene said, flashing Manny a smile, and continuing. "And I start at Columbia in graduate school creative writing next month. I'll need to find someplace to live here in the next couple of weeks. I've been going to the Philadelphia School of the Arts. They cover performing arts as well as fine arts and writing. I guess you can say I've had a smattering of training in several areas of the arts. Dancing and specific courses in modeling helped me get this job. I need to work while I'm at Columbia."

Gene had rested his forearm on the café table and Manny was running his fingers lightly up and down the skin of the young man's inner arms. God, this is easy, Manny thought again, not quite believing his luck. Gene wasn't pulling away from him.

"So you have to go back to Philadelphia today?" he said.

"There's a train tonight," Gene said. "I don't have any classes tomorrow."

"Maybe I can walk you."

"I think I can find Penn Station by myself," Gene said, with a smile.

"I wasn't thinking of walking you to Penn Station. I was thinking of walking you to my place. I live just over in Hells Kitchen from here, near 52nd and 9th Avenue."

"I'm glad that's what you meant," Gene said, with a smile.

"You know what I'm saying, though." This seemed too easy. Manny wanted to pin it down.

"You're saying you want to fuck me. I'm saying yes."

* * * *

Gene was lying on the bed on his back, his eyes wide and watering, his arms held over his head by Manny's strong grip on his wrists. Gene's fingers were wrapped around the rungs of the brass headboard. Manny straddled his chest, leaning over him, feeding his thick cock into Gene's mouth. Gene was writhing under him, gagging and groaning, not having been prepared for a cock as big as Manny's. But Manny relentlessly face fucked him, his cock engorging until he had come close to exploding. He didn't want to do that yet.

He released the young man's wrists, but Gene left his hands in place, gripping the rungs of the brass headboard as Manny moved down his body to where he was straddling Gene's thighs. He brought their cock heads together, his uncut and Gene's cut. He docked the cocks, pressing the bulbs together, pulling his foreskin over Gene's bulb, and stroked the cocks together as Gene moaned, arched his back and started to move his hips in the rhythm of the fuck

Now. Now, Gene was thinking. He was going to put it in him now and take him to heaven. "Now. Do it now," he murmured to egg the man on.

Easy was one thing. That didn't mean it had to be fast—that Manny couldn't savor the conquest, couldn't squeeze all of the pleasure he could get out of it before carving the notch in his bedpost. He continued docking the cocks.

It was Manny who dock fucked a release out of his captive first, pulling an ejaculation out of an overwhelmed Gene, not having experienced docking before, and laughing as Gene shuddered, jerked, and slathered both cock heads with his cum, which burbled out underneath the covering foreskin and dripped down Gene's shaft. The gorgeous little piece might be easy, but he was fresh. He hadn't become a jaded bottom yet.

Gene lay there, panting and moaning as Manny moved further down, placing his feet on the floor at the foot of the bed, and pulled Gene down to where his buttocks rested on the bottom edge of the mattress. Gene lost his grip on the headboard and reached down and ran his fingers into the hair on the back of Manny's head, holding Manny close into him, as the older man swallowed Gene's cock and eventually moved down and ate out his ass, opening him up to the thrust of the cock.

Gene lay there, wide-eyed and seemingly helpless, holding his legs raised and spread as Manny stood between his thighs, rolled on a condom, and spritzed his cock and Gene's hole with lube.

"Now. To it now," Gene murmured again.

Manny laughed. And then he was thrusting inside Gene's passage, deep, and immediately setting up a rhythm of the fuck that had Gene howling and writhing under him, clutching Manny's shoulders, digging in his fingernails there, and setting his own hips in a frenzied countermotion of pain-pleasure and moving up the scale of ecstasy.

Manny fucked him for a while in the missionary and then flipped him over on the bed, covered him close from above, and fucked him in a doggie, rising off his back, grabbing Gene's wrists, and arching him back as he thrust hard up into his passage. He finished the young model in a wheel barrow, sitting on the foot of the bed, with Gene's body cantilevered out from him, Gene's fists buried in the carpet and his legs wrapped around Manny's waist, and Manny pulling his passage on and off the cock, on and off the cock.

"You're such a slut for it," Manny said afterward as he sat, naked, on the bed and watched Gene dress. Manny wasn't going to walk the young model to Penn Station. He'd gotten what he wanted. He did tell Gene where the nearest subway stop was.

"Yeah, well, it's Sunday. I'm prim and proper on the weekdays," Gene answered.

"I could tell that it was still exciting for you, that you were hungry for it. You said you need to find a living situation—a roommate with an apartment, I trust."

"Yeah, I haven't decided whether I need to be close to Columbia, where I'll be studying, or down here in the garment district, where I'll have to work. The woman at the House of Havlos said I might be called on short order and if I can't show up right away I might lose the job. It's a long ride from Columbia."

"There's a Web site you could try to help you find a living arrangement," Manny said, writing the URL down on a slip of paper and handing it to Gene. "You were a good lay. I'm glad we met on a Sunday."

"I'm glad too," Gene said. "You're a bit scary and intense, but I really got my rocks off, which is what I wanted." And then, fully dressed again, he left.

Back in Philadelphia the next day and without a class to go to, Gene went up on the Internet to check out the Web site Manny had told him about. It was obviously a gay male hookup site, concentrated on New York City. It did include a bulletin board on roommates and apartments, though. He found what appeared to be the ideal match for his needs in living accommodations in New York.

"Share near the garment district," it said, "One dominant, totally in-shape thirty-two-year-old seeking one small, slim sub. Cost depending on the quality and frequency of servicing." Pretty straightforward and boldly worded, Gene thought. But, depending on what this thirty-two-year-old dominant seeker looked like, it could be ideal. The thought of a discounted rent was very appealing, and Gene had already decided he would need to be close to the garment district, at least until his modeling reputation grew to where his needs would be accommodated.

He messaged the e-mail address and set up a meet on the steps of the New York Public Library, facing Bryant Park, for the next Sunday afternoon.

Of course the New York apartment was the one he'd been in already the previous Sunday, the thirty-two-year-old dominator was Manny Rodriguez, and the bed Manny fucked him on and was advertising to use was the same one he'd been fucked on the week before.

"Your share of the rent would be $600 a month," Manny said. "But it would be discounted each time you took my cock during that month. Deal?"

That would be no more than twelve times a month to live close to the garment district rent free, Gene quickly calculated.

"Deal," he said.

"First hundred dollars discounted today," Manny said. "Fifty dollars for the fuck we just did and fifty for the one I'm now going to take."

Gene groaned as Manny rolled over on top of him again, but he opened his legs to the man and took the thrust of the cock deep.

It was Sunday.

* * * *

Sunday in the park. Central Park that was. Gene picked it because it was close to a lot of high-end hotels, ones where out-of-town businessmen checked in to in anticipation of early morning meetings on Monday. There always were businessmen who liked to let loose when they were in New York and out of the clutches of their suburban lives, with a wife, two-and-a-half children, a dog, and a cat. And there were men who liked to indulge in entirely different preferences than the life they lived in public when they were in a large, impersonal town like New York. The Las Vegas "What plays in Vegas, stays in Vegas" creed applied to other large cities as well.

The runway gigs weren't coming fast enough yet, the costs of starting up a graduate program were high, and Manny wasn't so demanding that there wasn't some rent to pay. It was Sunday. Gene was making ends meet—at least temporarily, he hoped—by turning a trick or two in the park on Sunday.

It hadn't been hard. He was a real looker, moved like a dancer, and looked young, fresh, and vulnerable. Mostly all he had to do was sit on a bench not far from a drinks truck near the edge of Central Park. He could count on a seeking businessman to come along and maybe pass him three times, giving him increasingly meaningful smiles until Gene gave a shy smile, widened his stance, let his hand glide down onto his basket for the brief moment the mark was passing, and dip his head. That was usually all he need do to acquire interested company. He could be discriminating. He could signal availability only to men he could see himself going with. Being in the fashion business, he was more interested in the quality and apparent expense of the clothes than in the man's physique, although that had to be acceptable too.

He probably was willing to go with someone older and heftier then most, though—if he had good and expensive taste in clothing. He reasoned that a man with money was best for a one-time Sunday trick than a pretty boy who you'd normally ball for free—and likely would expect you to this time as well.

On this Sunday, the man was expensively dressed, he was a bit jowly and thick around the middle, and he was on the dark side of fifty, but he turned out to be quite satisfactory. He had a great hotel room, a fat wallet, and a thick cock, and he knew how to make best use of all of that.

He bent Gene over an expansive bed beside a full-length and width window overlooking the park, covered him from behind and above and rode Gene's ass like the winning jockey at Belmont with a demanding, beer-can category cock. Gene's cries of pain-pleasure—more genuine than was often the case—were muffled by his silk briefs stuffed in his mouth, and the john let Gene clutch the $300 fee in his hand while he was pounding his ass. Coming into the home stretch, the man moved Gene to his back, and finished him in a raised-hips missionary position. There was a mirrored wall on the other side of the bed, and Gene was able to admire his lithe, stretched-out body, with his pelvis raised and the man's cock moving in and out of his ass for the finale.

Gene was walking gingerly, but steeped in satisfaction, when he returned to the apartment. He normally would have been playing the street until dark, but the hefty jockey had ridden and paid him well and he was home earlier than usual.

He had returned earlier than Manny had expected him. The naked man sitting on Manny's bed with two light towers pointed at him from across the room wasn't what Gene expected Manny would be bringing home. He was a black bull—muscular and hung. It was doubtful he was a bottom and Manny had shown no indication that he played defense as well as offense.

The black bull gave Gene a look like he could eat him alive when Gene entered the room with a questioning look on his face.

"You're home early," Manny said. He was standing at one of the light towers, adjusting something. A video camera rested on the floor by his feet. "Maybe that's a good thing," he added.

"I got lucky early," Gene answered. "What's all this then? And why might my coming home early be a good thing?"

"We were going to film a movie here," Manny said. "The bottom called and canceled. I haven't been able to find a replacement."

"And, so, what does that mean?" Gene asked.

The black bull fucked the stuffing out of Gene for the movie, forcing the small-stature model to kneel to him and gag on his massive cock and then threw him on the bed, raised him to all fours, mounted him, stuffed his ass, and rode him and rode him and rode him. All of this was done under the lights and to the whir of the video camera held by Manny as he circled the room taking the shot at the best angle of the moment.

It turned out that their apartment was also a studio for gay male porn videos and Gene wasn't aware of that that until one of the actors had failed to appear for that day's shoot and Gene got home earlier than anticipated. Gene agreed to stand in—or, rather, lie in with his legs open—when he found out that he'd earn a flat $500 up front and another $500 when and if a porn site bought the film. It was a coupling randy men salivated over—a black bull conquering a sweet young thing—so Manny convinced Gene it would be a sure $1,000.

Gene needed the money, and it was Sunday.

Later, as he was editing the film, Manny said, "This is a sure winner . . ." which it was. "We'll need a stage name for you to put in the trailer and to pimp to the porn sites."

"How about Will Belayed?" Gene shot back flippantly.

"Great. Done," Manny answered and burned the name into the film credits.

* * * *

It was on a Sunday in Central Park that Gene realized that Victor Macek, a man Gene had come to worship enough that he was researching the Serbian nationalist movement to take a shot at writing a romantic adventure novel featuring Macek, was a gay boy shopper. Gene had been working the park long enough to know most of the other young men who did the same. Gene had developed a nodding acquaintance with a young guy near his own age, Alonzo, who was a "back of the front line" sometimes dancer in Broadway shows and who made ends meet much the same way Gene was doing in working Central Park.

That Sunday Gene was walking into the park when he realized he was walking a good distance behind one of his night class visiting lecturers at Columbia, the novelist and Serbian nationalist Victor Macek. The man taught political novel writing at Columbia, and Gene had become entranced not only with how hunky the man was in person but also how dangerously and romantically adventuresome were the events he wrote about in the breakup of Eastern Europe and the sectarian infighting there. He was a rugged, thuggish, hard-used-looking man, probably in his early, experienced forties, who was ugly and handsome at the same time. His battle scars showed on his face and his muscular body was powerfully built and, in addition to imagining writhing under him, Gene could fantasize about tracing the scars of other wounds on his body while being taxed with what he was sure was a thick cock in his passage.

Gene was highly sexed enough to gauge each man he met as a possible lover. His political novel class professor at Columbia ranked high on Gene's list of possible lovers—and not just as a lover but as a rough, demanding dominator. The thought of sex with the man both scared and fascinated Gene. There were times when

Gene wanted to be manhandled. That was one reason he played the Central Park game. He'd been told to watch out for johns picked up there—that often a mild-looking upper-upper-middle-class businessman shopped there to let loose of his inner nasty. On occasion that was what Gene was looking for in a hookup.

Gene followed Macek, thinking of a way that he could get to his bench before the hunky Serbian would pass that way. At first he thought the man was meandering, but he eventually could see that he was stalking—that he was following the rent-boy Alonzo. Alonzo must have sensed that too, because he found a bench, sat, and let Macek slow as he passed him—then he went into slow, eye-contact motion for two more passes before he sat on the bench beside the young dancer, who had held his ground on the bench. Gene watched them leave the park together, Macek cupping the dancer's buttocks and leading him in the direction of 7th Avenue.

Later that afternoon Gene encountered Alonzo in the park.

"I saw the john you left with earlier, the rough-looking guy with the great build," Gene said. "Was he—?"

"I'd suggest staying away from him," Alonzo interjected. "Rough, intense bastard. Big dicked, and it was all about him. He didn't fuck as much as he conquered. Really rough."

"But he did it for you?"

"He paid well . . . yes."

"I mean, you got totally fucked?"

"I got totally beaten down and ravished."

Gene shivered. Alonzo obviously had meant it as a turn-away warning, but Gene was in a mood and it hit him more as a delicious arousal. So impressed was he that, when the opportunity came, he forgot his rule of only really letting loose on Sunday.

The next Tuesday night he went to his political novels class at Columbia twitching and hardly able to concentrate on the lecture. Macek seemed to be preoccupied and lost his place in his notes several times too—and he seemed to let his eyes linger on Gene more than on most in the class. He asked that Gene stay late after class.

"Your class project prospectus says you were working on a novel about the violence in the breakup of Yugoslavia, Gene," he said to the young man at the desk in front of the room while the other students were filing out.

"Yes, I find that period fascinating and . . ." He didn't complete the sentence. He would have said "arousing." That's what he thought about the topic, brought on, he knew, by how he viewed the hunky, mysterious Serbian nationalist who was teaching this course. He couldn't be open about that, though. In his fantasies he wanted to be writhing under this man, but he was a teacher. Gene knew it would be dangerous to go there—even now when he knew that Macek played the Central Park game.

"I was there—in Yugoslavia—during the breakup. I could give you some pointers that might help you decide where to begin with your work."

"Could you? That would be terrific," Gene said.

"This evening. Now. We could go to a café or hotel bar or somewhere and chat a bit for an hour. I have time. What do you think?"

It was the bar in a small, rather seedy hotel a few blocks from the Columbia campus, entered off a dark side street. There weren't many others in the bar. All of them were men. As he sipped his drink and before anything was said other than innocuous chitchat, Gene watched a middle-aged man in a suit pick up a young guy in tight jeans and a chest-revealing mesh T-shirt who had been perched on a stool at the end of the bar. They didn't head for the hotel exit when they left the bar; they went together to the bank of elevators to the upper floors. So, it was that kind of hotel.

Macek didn't even get into talking about Yugoslavia and Serbian nationalism.

"I saw you in the park—in Central Park—on Sunday," he said.

"It's not too far from where I live," Gene answered. "I like to go there for inspiration."

"I'm well aware of why young men like you go there," Macek said, putting a hand under the surface of the table and gripping Gene's knee. Gene wanted to yelp from how strong the grip was, but he also wanted to melt. He started going hard. "I've also seen a couple of the videos you've been in."

"Videos?" Gene asked, panicked about whether to admit to them or not.

"They are on the Internet, on some of the Web sites I like to check out. You're a sexy young man," Macek said in a husky voice. "I want to fuck you. I want to break you—like I've seen a black bodybuilder do to you on film, but more so."

"I, uh . . ."

"I have a room upstairs."

Of course he did. It wasn't Sunday, and Gene had a rule that he didn't let loose to his fantasies like this except on Sunday, but, God, he wanted this.

Macek was rough and violent and fucked Gene totally, and the young man hated and loved it, lying there on the floor of the seedy hotel room in a fetal position, mentally checking out both the surface and internal damage when the Serb had dressed and left the room—and still half hoping that the door would open and the man would return and continue using his body to its limits.

No man Gene had had sex with until now had a cock the size of Macek's, and no man had used his cock as a weapon like Macek had done with him. If Gene hadn't been promiscuous and trained to big cocks, the Serb would have totally ruined him.

The first fuck was just inside the room, starting with Gene on his knees and Macek brutally face fucking him while he took short time outs to strip the young man. Macek remained clothed, just his long, heavy dick protruding out of his fly. He lifted the moaning Gene, turned him, and slammed him up against the wall next to the door.

"Chest and cheek against the wall; butt projected out," he commanded, and Gene did as commanded. Grabbing Gene's wrists together with one strong hand, Macek forced the young man's arms above his head. Guiding his cock with the other hand, he put it in position at Gene's ass, spit down on his cock a couple of times to provide a minimum off lube, and, as Gene cried out at the violation, penetrated him deep and began to pump hard.

It took Gene much huffing and puffing and watering of the eyes to open to the man, but when he had and Macek had set up a steady rhythm of the fuck, the Serb suddenly pulled out of Gene's ass, spun him around, and gave him a slap across the face that sent the young man reeling back to go down on his belly on the bed. Macek was immediately straddling him and pulling strips of leather from around his waist that had served as a belt. He used these to bind Gene's wrists, his arms extended above his head, the young man's ankles, and his legs, holding his thighs close together.

"Is this how you treated your enemies in Serbia?" Gene asked, close to sobbing.

"Yes, but you are not my enemy. You will survive it. But you want to write about how brutal the civil wars were where I came from? This is a taste of that. If I had not done it, it would have been done to me."

Macek stood off from the side of the bed, giving Gene a full view of him, while he stripped. His body was muscular, magnificent. And there were scars on his torso and thighs from the grazing of bullets and knife slashes. When he turned his back, Gene could see permanent welts from lashings. Gene moaned and whimpering, having no trouble understanding what the man had been through and what had made him so demanding and violent.

And then Gene screamed, which was muffled by Macek stuffing Gene's briefs in his mouth. The Serb had mounted his ass on the bed, had thrust inside his restricted passage with his huge cock, and was pumping him again.

Gene's senses were flooded with a combination of pain and pleasure. This was what he'd been aching for—to feel the fuck. He'd been with so many "slam-bang-thanks-good-bye" men in the last couple of months that this hell was heaven for him. The cum rose quickly in him and he shot his load into the bedspread on the creaking bed.

With a laugh, Macek whipped off the bindings and turned Gene and pushed him off to the floor.

"Crawl to the door," he commanded. "Let's see how far you get."

Gene didn't get far before Macek reached him; crouched over him, holding him up on all fours; and finished the fuck doggie style, taking him from behind and above hard and deep. When the Serb had ejaculated, he tore off his condom, dropped it in front of Gene's face, and let the young man collapse into a fetal position.

"That was fun," he growled as he dressed. "You've got a sweet, tight ass. Surprising as much as you've probably been used. You gave in to it like you really wanted it. You needed it and you loved it. We'll do it again. You'll make great grades in the course—and you'll be surprised where we meet again." And then he left the room.

The young man lay there, moaning, too weak even to pull the briefs out of his mouth for some time. He had been brutalized. He ached all over. But he was in heaven. The man had been right. It was exactly what he had needed. The question was how often could he take what he now knew he needed and still survive?

* * * *

Not all men picked up in Central Park were rough or self-possessed and one trick Gene served in the weeks Victor Macek was reeling him in under his control remained memorable in Gene's mind. Gene was lounging on his usual bench in the park. Sometime previously he had noticed a possible john sitting on a bench across the path and a bit down from Gene's bench. The man was obviously Jewish, complete with black yarmulke—a small skull cap— white shirt and black trousers, and was at least in his late thirties, but he looked like he had a good body and he had a sultry sensuality about him. He had a bushy, wavy head of black hair, which also curled on his bare forearms and spilled out of the neck of his white shirt, the top two buttons open and the fineness of the shirt material not obscuring the hairy barrel chest underneath.

Gene caught the man watching him, and he wondered why he was taking so long to approach him if he was looking for a rent-boy. But he wasn't just watching. He was sketching on a large pad of paper as well. Gene was wondering whether he was expected to make the approach, when the rent-boy, Alonzo, who he knew from working the park, strolled by, stopped, and stood in front of the bench, raising one foot after the other, placing them beside Gene, to stretch out his legs. He and Gene chatted a bit.

Gene brought Alonzo's attention to the Jewish man at the bench across the way. "See that guy across the path? He's been sitting there sketching and watching me for some time. You know anything about him? Is he a player."

Alonzo looked around, took the man in, and turned back and smiled. "That's the lover."

"The lover?"

"Yeah. His name is Josh—a rich Jew from the garment district. He's one who's good for you on a day you've been fucked really rough. He's sweet. He'll make you believe in riding the clouds in sex. Hung like a bull but he makes love—doesn't just fuck. Pays well."

After Alonzo moved on, Gene waited a few minutes, giving the guy he'd called "the lover" time to either make a move or move on, but he didn't do either. So, Gene made the move himself.

"Hi. I couldn't help seeing you over here, looking at me and sketching something," Gene said, standing in front of the man where he was sitting on the bench. The man gave him a warm smile.

"I was sketching you," the man said. "I'm in men's wear. You look like a male model. I couldn't resist drawing you in some clothes I've been designing in my mind." He flipped a couple of pages on his sketch pad and turned it to where Gene could see it.

"Hey. That's really good. It looks like me. And you thought right. I *am* a male model. I like what you've clothed me in in that sketch. I think you should make that ensemble."

"I've also been wondering what else you might do," the man said. "Do you do anything else other than modeling? I saw you talking with Alonzo just now. Do you do what Alonzo does?"

"Go with men for money, do you mean?"

"Yes. Alonzo has gone with me."

"That's what he said."

"Did he say he was disappointed with going with me?"

"No. He was very complimentary."

"I haven't just sketched you in clothes I'm considering designing," the man said. "I also like to sketch fantasies I have. Would you like to see? You probably don't want to see it if you aren't cruising."

"Sure, I'd love to see it," Gene answered.

The man flipped the pages in the sketch pad again and turned another sketch around for Gene to see.

Gene sucked in breath. The sketch was of two men—he and the man—this man, Josh. Both of them were naked. The man in the sketch was fucking Gene in a missionary on a bed. The man in the sketch had a beautiful, hirsute body. He was holding the other man's hips and he was inside him deep. Gene of the sketch had his legs raised and spread and his head was arched back looking at the viewer. The expression on his face was one of ecstasy.

"Is this how Alonzo said it would be with me?" the man whispered.

"Yes," Gene said, with a low moan. "How realistic is this sketch you've done of yourself?"

"I try to be honest in my sketching. Would you go with me for the night if you find I look like this naked? My place is a couple of subway stops away. Will you go with me and then lay down for me if I live up to this sketch?" He named a fee that was quite generous.

They hopped a subway at the 72nd Street station midway at the park on West Central Park and rode it down to the port authority stop at 42nd Street. The Jew, introducing himself as Josh, held Gene's eyes with his during the journey, but he didn't otherwise touch him or show evidence of possession or dominance. They chatted a bit, Josh revealing that he ran an exclusive men's shop, designing and showing his own clothes to an invitation-only list of well-heeled patrons. Beyond that he also volume edited a small literary journal. Their interests were amazingly similar, despite the difference in the worlds they lived in. Although Josh was in the modern tradition, he was definitely a traditional Jew, if not extremely Orthodox, and was right at home in the garment district world. Gene had been raised totally unchurched. Because of their expressed mutual interests, Gene revealed more of himself than he normally would to a john. He told Josh of his modeling for the House of Havlos and that he was a creative writing student at Columbia.

Their destination was a narrow, five-story brownstone on a quiet block of 39th Street, smack dab in the middle of the garment district, the ground floor of which had a garage door at one side that, Josh said, led back to several parking spaces across the back of building to accommodate his personal car and a couple of shop vans, and a shop on the other side, with large windows toward the street with mannequins, in men's clothes, on display. Between them was a door and a hallway with an elevator and a stairwell beyond.

As they waited for the elevator, Josh pulled Gene gently to him and they engaged in their first, tender kiss. "That was nice," Josh whispered as the elevator arrived and they pulled away from each other. "You have sweet, soft lips."

Yes, it was nice, Gene agreed in his mind.

As the elevator rose, Josh pointed out what they were passing. The second floor was for the clothing business work rooms. The third was where his literary magazine was published. The fourth and fifth proved to house Josh's expansive, expensively and tastefully furnished living quarters. Alonzo had told Gene Josh was from money. Gene believed him.

Josh's technique was to work slowly but deliberately and always with the climax anticipated, and it worked a charm with Gene, who was used to the fast lay and faster good-bye.

The bottom floor of Josh's living quarters was essentially all one room, with one area flowing into the other and the back wall, overlooking a flood-light swathed lush garden, being entirely glass. The seduction sofa faced the wall of glass, so that when Josh went to the kitchen area marked off with a breakfast bar island to make their drinks, Gene didn't see him.

When he came back with drinks, he had stripped down to a pair of filmy white cotton nearly knee-length boxer shorts. The shorts might have been from a line of sexy men's clothes designed by Josh himself, as they were cleverly constructed to give dueling impressions. On the surface they were very modest, covering a lot and looking like dowdy puritanical undergarments. But as Gene saw when Josh was standing before him, holding out Gene's drink, they were so gauzy that they were functionally transparent.

Josh was dark haired and hirsute. He was built solid and muscular without being overbuilt. The patterns of curls on his forearms and thighs and swirling around his pecs and down his sternum and belly and into his pubes were so sensual that they had to be groomed. The curls of his pubes were also tight but manly. Most significant, they could clearly be seen through the material of the underwear. His half-hard cock was mammoth, the exposed bulb huge and pressed against the material of the cotton shorts, hiding nothing while declaring the garb as pure innocence.

Josh looked down into Gene's eyes. "Satisfactory? Does it live up the sketch?"

"Very satisfactory," Gene whispered in a breathy voice. In his mind he was already riding the juicy cock.

But Josh made him wait.

* * * *

They sat close to each other on the sofa, looking out into the garden as the natural light floated away to be replaced by the spotlights highlighting new and different aspects. They sipped their drinks and kissed and fondled each other, Josh's hands going everywhere, slowly disrobing Gene until the young man was naked and hard and throbbing. Josh brushed Gene's hand away each time he tried to remove the gauzy underwear shorts, the last of what Josh was wearing, but he didn't stop the man he'd bought for the night from slipping his hand under the garment's waistband and fondling Josh's balls and stroking his cock bigger and bigger and bigger yet.

An album rested on the coffee table. Gene had assumed that it would contain dirty photos meant to arouse him. But, even better, it contained sketches rendered by Josh himself of other young men—and of Josh—of Josh fucking other young men on this sofa or on a bed, mostly likely in a room above where they were plastered together, making languid love, working their way into higher heat and arousal. Invariably in the sketches, the young man was shown in ecstasy. In some the root of Josh's thick cock was shown inside the young man's gaping hole. Josh was giving Gene every opportunity to know the extraordinary length and girth of him, so Gene's arousal of knowing how much of Josh was inside the young men in these sketches—and the anticipation that they were moving slowly but inexorably to the shaft being inside Gene heightened his arousal to where he couldn't take any more.

Josh broke the tension by pulling away from Gene and standing in front of him, his thumbs under the edge of the waistband of the shorts on either side, at his hips, his face smiling, inviting, commanding. *He* wasn't going to do it; Gene had to pull them away. He did, and the massive erection popped out of him. He took it in his mouth and gagged at the attempt to handle it all, while Josh stood there in front of him, murmuring what he liked and what he liked better, his hips swaying slowly, his fingers pinching and rubbing his own nipples, face fucking his young man for the night.

After an eternity, Josh gripped Gene's shoulders with his hands and gently pushed the young man back into the sofa, twisting his body so that his chest was pressed into the sofa arm. He reached around and picked up the album again, turning the pages to show the sketch of another young man draped over the sofa arm, his knees pressed into the edge of the sofa cushion, and his tail in the air. Josh was hovering over the young man, holding his massive cock in his hand up to the young man's hole. The page was flipped and another young man was in the same position, but Josh was cupping his chin, arching his head back, the young man's mouth was open in a silent scream, and Josh's shaft was buried to the hilt inside his ass. The third sketch was yet another young man in the same position about to be skewered, and the fourth, another sketch of the cock buried.

Gene was breathing heavily and panting. He elevated his tail, moving into the position of the young men being fucked in the sketches. "Fuck me, fuck me. Fuck me now," he whimpered. They had moved beyond the male whore and john stage into one man wanting to be covered by the other one. This was what Josh had been waiting for.

Josh mounted the sofa and Gene's ass and did just that, slowly, sensually, totally.

Later, after feeding him a steak dinner, Josh fucked Gene again in a large bed in a room immediately above the living room sofa—and with a full glass wall onto the lighted garden. He took an hour and a half with Gene, slowly, totally bringing Gene to the brink in demanding positions and then holding, deep inside him, waiting for the young man to come away from an explosion before starting to work him again to a high level of pleasure and arousal. Three times Gene shot his load before Josh could stave his completion off, but Josh just laughed each time and began again.

At the end of the hour and a half, having gone late into the night, Gene dozed off, totally exhausted and satiated, lying on his belly, one leg and one arm dangling off the side of the bed, with Josh half covering him on the other side, nibbling at an ear lobe and still working Gene's prostate with a buried index finger.

In the morning he lay there, after having ridden Josh's cock in a cowboy, and watched Josh shower in a glass-fronted cubicle and then dress for the day in his shop downstairs.

"I'm afraid I'm late." You'll have to see yourself out after you've showered and dressed.

"Will we do this again?" Gene asked. "You may have been the best I've had."

"Are you fishing for a rating from me?" Josh said, giving Gene a half smile and an amused look in his eyes.

"No, of course not . . . yes."

"Let's say that I won't pay you for sex again."

"Oh, I'm sorry I didn't satisfy," Gene said, his disappointment clear in his voice.

"Oh, you satisfied fully. But it cheapens it for me to pay you for it. You satisfied me so much that I could see you as a lover, not as a paid whore. Think about it. If you want to see it as a possible relationship, come back to me again. If not, I don't want it to be something tawdry."

"Quite aside from that," Josh said, "you said that you are writing in your graduate studies—fiction, using the breakup of Yugoslavia as a setting, did you say? Intriguing. Bring me some of your writing. We're always looking for new writers for my literary journal."

He left, leaving Gene to think of what he wanted. Alonzo had been right, Josh had been a lover. Victor Macek was a master, a conqueror. Which did Gene want? Could he get both?

But as for sending something Josh might use in his literary journal? Certainly. Someday he would be notable for his writing, not for opening his legs to randy men.

* * * *

Victor Macek didn't care about Gene Worth's whoring only on Sunday policy. Indeed, the young man didn't have the courage to tell Macek there was such a policy. For the next three weeks, Macek took Gene to the seedy hotel near the campus after the Tuesday evening class and banged the shit out of him. He wasn't as brutal with him as he had been the first time, but he took him hard in every position that occurred to him, and Gene gave him whatever he wanted. Each time it was a victor taking the spoils and doing so brutally. Macek paid him, though, and told him to stay out of the park on Sunday—to save it all for him—and Gene did what the Serb thug told him to do. Gene was totally submissive to the hunky Serb, who fucked him totally every Tuesday night.

Gene didn't have much left for Manny Rodriguez and the two drifted apart, Gene spending as much time at the Columbia library and pestering the model assignment assistant at the House of Havlos for work as he did in Manny's apartment. Although Manny pressured him to do more porn films, Gene held these off as well. He had been shocked that Macek had seen a couple of them and recognized him. Gene hadn't fully thought out what happened to those films.

It was to avoid being in the apartment while Manny was filming one Sunday evening that prompted Gene to attend a faculty-student cocktail party on the Columbia campus, where his life took a sudden and significant turn.

Victor Macek drifted over to him, a glass of beer in hand to give him, as Gene was entering the party room.

32

"I'm glad you came," Macek said in a low voice. "I was going to tell you to but it slipped my mind. I have a proposal for you."

"A proposal? I had to get out of my apartment. I thought coming here was as good as anywhere," Gene answered. "And there's free beer," he said, lifting the glass Macek had given him.

"So, Rodriguez is filming another porn scene you didn't want to be in?"

Gene gave the Serb a shocked look. He'd never told him Manny Rodriguez was his roommate, let alone that he's the one who filmed the porn videos. He hadn't told Macek anything at all about Manny. "Excuse me. How did you—?"

"I told you I'd seen the films. Manny is the one who showed them to me. But hold that thought. I have others to talk to. But, before I go, didn't you tell me once that you fucked women too."

"Yes, sometimes, but—"

"And you'd do it for advantage and if our own arrangement could be more convenient?"

"Probably, but—"

But Macek heard his name being called from across the room, and he turned from Gene and was moving away between clumps of people chattering and laughing. A student Gene had a couple of classes with slid into the space were Macek had been and started talking to Gene.

Macek was gone before Gene realized that he hadn't said what the proposal he had was—and why he had asked whether Gene fucked women too.

While he chatted with the other student, Gene's eyes roamed the room, looking for Macek. When he saw him, he froze and a chill went up his spine.

"I wonder why that woman over there is here?" he said, "the older woman talking with Macek."

"Oh, that's his wife," the other student answered. "She some sort of fashion house queen over in the garment district."

The chill went up his spine again. It wasn't because he had been told the woman worked in the fashion industry. He knew that. It was Helene Havlos, the head of the House of Havlos, the fashion house he modeled for. He'd caught glimpses of her before—and had seen her looking at him, as well. What caused him to do a double take was learning that there was a connection between her—from where he worked—and Victor Macek—from where he went to school. The woman who controlled his paycheck and the man who not only controlled his success in school but who was fucking him. It couldn't get any more dangerous than this. He couldn't help himself; he felt himself going hard. The danger of it was intoxicating.

Later Macek came back to Gene when he was alone.

"Come with me. You need to go to the men's room," he said, coming up close to Gene and putting a hand on the small of Gene's back—possessively, although not in sight of anyone in the room.

"I do?" Gene asked. But when Macek pressed in with his hand, indicating a direction in which he wanted Gene to go, the young man stood his ground. "You didn't tell me you were married to Helene Havlos," he said. "You don't know I work for her—that I do some modeling for her fashion house?"

"Of course I know. And I know about the videos because Manny Rodriguez brought them to me. Manny does work for her too. I thought I'd be interested in you and he knew you were one of my students. He pimps for me now and again. He was right. I wanted to fuck you even before he showed me the videos. I want to fuck you now. Come to the men's room with me."

Gene's anger at Manny flared up. He was even more of a manipulating pimp than Gene had known. Gene was just someone for him to use for his own advantage.

"Wait. You said you had a proposal for me. Tell me. Does it have anything to do with whether I'd fuck a woman?"

"Yes it does. Helene and I have a good relationship, but I don't fuck her. She likes her male models. The one she has had in her bed has left her for a Paris house."

"Nikos? Nikos Constandinos?"

"Yes, the very one. She's had her eye on you. You could write your ticket for modeling gigs and up your fee scale. She's quite a load, but she's not disgusting. And once you're fused with her she'll drain you dry and you'll have a good enough time. The deal is you come to live with us in our apartment on Central Park West, by the park—it's big enough that we rattle around in it—and you'll get free room and board and cash on the side when you perform. And the bonus is that I'll be there to use and pay you when she isn't. What do you say?"

"Well, I—"

"I'm not going to wait around for you to mull it. My balls ache. I'm going to fuck you. Come with me."

Gene went with him, through one corridor off the party room and then turning into another. It wasn't a communal men's room. It was a private bathroom. Macek slammed Gene's back against the wall and unbuckled, unzipped, and jerked the young man's trousers in one deft move. He took two condom packets out of his pocket, slit one, removed the disk, and rolled it onto Gene's hard cock.

"What is this? You want me to—?"

"No, of course I don't want you to fuck me. I'm fucking you, and I'm going to do you so hard, you'll come a gusher for me. I don't want this to get messy. We have to go back to the party."

Still pushing against Gene with his chest to hold the young man against the wall, he unzipped himself, stripped the trousers of both of them down to the floor, growled for Gene to step out of his and he did the same, and then he rolled the other condom on his cock.

"Climb my hips with your legs," he growled.

Gene did so, grunted and panted as Macek spiked him, and then they were both groaning and moaning, as Macek pushed Gene's back up and down on the wall with the strength of the thrusts of his cock and bruised Gene's lips with his kisses.

Gene came a gusher into the condom covering his shaft just as promised and Macek wasn't long behind him.

As they readjusted their clothing, Macek said, "If you come live with us and keep Helene happy, in addition to room and board and incidentals she'll pay you $200 for every jack off like that and I'll pay you $100 when you do it for me. I'll make you happier so I won't pay you as much. So, how about it?"

The duplicity of his current roommate flashed through his brain as did the unlikelihood that he'd have to go back out into Central Park anytime soon. Colder weather was coming on.

"OK, fine."

* * * *

The West Central Park apartment proved to be even larger and more lavishly appointed than Gene had imagined it would be. It took up half of the eighteenth floor of a converted early twentieth-century hotel. The apartment was fully staffed with phantom servants, bar one. Except for that one, they went about their duties unobtrusively and effectively. The staff of the head of the House of Havlos included—if you didn't count her husband, Victor, and now Gene—a cook, a housekeeper, a butler/handyman, a chauffeur, and a lady's maid. All of them saw everything but made like they saw nothing, and they all efficiently cleaned up anything that was out of order without judgment. The one exception was Helene's hairdresser and makeup artist. Leon was a nervous little French male tart who hated Gene the minute Gene took up residence and let him know that he did.

Gene sensed that from the start and he only had to speculate about why it was so to the middle of first night.

Helene celebrated Gene's addition to the household by summoning him to her bed that first night. She didn't want the young man to stay the night—only long enough for her to coax an ejaculation out of him and to make sure he could satisfactorily service her. She had passed seventy and was what those currying favor with her called zaftig. The fact is that she was one hefty old lady. She had big jugs for tits; beyond that just about everything else was too big too. Her cunt was a cavern guarded by puffy lips. She looked younger, but at seventy-two that didn't necessarily mean much. She, of course, dressed elegantly and, having her own fashion house, managed to wear clothes that covered a lot. But a boy toy in her bed, fucking her, was going to know what couldn't be hidden.

Gene had been warned that she wasn't as interested in climaxes of her own as she was in the illusion that she could still pull them out of a young man—someone of the caliber, in desirable looks, of her male models. Thus Gene had to employ independent thoughts while he was mounting her in the semidarkness of her bedroom to manage to harden and come for her. Luckily, he was highly sexed and had a vivid imagination.

On that night Gene could switch between memories of sex alternately with her husband, Victor Macek, and the Jewish lover, Josh Steinem. And he managed. She was happy, after toying with his cock and fondling his body and even giving him some shaft mouth work, while being bent over several pillows on her bed on her belly and Gene covering her on top high, like a jockey, with his fists buried in the mattress on either side of her upper arms and crouched on her bent legs beside her thighs and riding her cunt. He established a good angle, good depth, and a lively bounce thanks to the leverage he could get off the balls of his feet. By alternating between thoughts of Victor's rough takings and Josh's lovemaking, Gene managed an ejaculation. She said there was no need for a condom, so she knew when he came and was pleased that, young and virile, he had a lot to give.

She was happy, and Gene tired her. So, she released him with a satisfied smile.

Gene's passage in the night hours to his own bedroom in the back depths of the warren of rooms in the apartment took the young man past Victor's bedroom. His door was slightly open. He had the hairdresser, Leon, on his knees at the foot of his bed, with his arms spread and bound to the thick posts of the four-poster bed. Both Victor and Leon were naked. Leon was writhing but egging Victor on as Victor strapped Leon's back and buttocks with a belt. Gene stood there in shock long enough to see Victor saddle up behind Leon, shove his hard cock up Leon's passage, and start to vigorously fuck him.

Later that night Victor visited Gene in his room to welcome the young man to the apartment. He took Gene in a vigorous, but mostly conventional missionary position, though, and there was only that one coupling that night, Victor having already gotten his rocks off with the hairdresser. At no time in the months Victor fucked Gene, although he fucked the young man rough, did he go to the extremes that he went with Leon. Leon didn't have to walk the catwalk in House of Havlos clothes and Gene did. Marks on a model's back would preclude him from working, and Gene had been promised more, not fewer, modeling gigs with this arrangement.

Leon, however, apparently loved it and was high strung and jealous. He knew Victor was doing Gene too—that Gene wasn't only in the apartment for Helene—and from the very beginning he hated the young model and was testy with Victor for fucking Gene too.

For a couple of months, Gene juggled attentions from Victor and Josh. He'd sent samples of his writing to Josh who professed to judge they were quite acceptable for publishing in his literary magazine. Josh used them to lure Gene back to his building and his bed again and again and to show Gene the ecstasy of intense lovemaking.

"You could come live with me—have a piece of producing the literary magazine and also model my clothes for me," Josh told Gene the last time the young man came to him for sex and strokes on his writing.

There came the night that everything changed, however.

Leon was supposed to be on vacation, so Victor had brought Gene into his bed for the night. Leon had missed his flight, and after hours of being unable to get on another one, he'd come back into the city, to the apartment.

When he walked past the door to Victor's bedroom, he found that it was ajar. Victor was on his back on the bed and he was holding Gene over him in the position of the crab, both men facing up to the ceiling, Gene supporting his back over Victor's chest with his arms bent and his fists buried in the mattress on either side of Victor's biceps, his legs bent and his feet flat on the mattress on either side of Victor's thighs, and Victor grasping his waist and raising and lowering the young man's ass channel on his cock.

It only took Leon a couple of seconds to grasp what was happening and for it to make his blood boil. He already was in a state from having his flight canceled and not being accommodated yet on a new flight. He went to his room, retrieved a revolver, and came back to Victor's bedroom door. When Leon started yelling obscenities at Gene for fucking *his* man, Victor moved to roll out from underneath Gene as the first shots were fired. In the process Gene was thrown off to one side before the bullets flew. The first three bullets caught Victor in the chest. The fourth one went into Leon's skull when he turned the gun on himself.

The story featured on the front page of the *New York Times* for three days. The distraught widow nearly had an emotional breakdown and required the total support of those nearest to her. There wasn't anyone nearer to her at that point than Gene Worth was. He became her constant companion at home and at work, having little time for anything else, although he somehow managed to finish out his semester at Columbia, receiving an A in the class Victor Macek had taught, based on the grades Macek had given before the jealous French hairdresser blew him away.

Chapter Two: New Orleans Sunday

He was being careful with her. Helene was bent over the foot of the king-sized bed in the bedroom alcove of her twelfth-floor Crescent City Suite at the New Orleans Marriott on Canal Street in the French Quarter, and the young male model, Gene Worth, was bent over her from behind. His hands were under her, cupping her pendulous breasts and working her nipples with their quarter-sized aureoles. Helene Havlos was proud of her large breasts and particularly liked it when Gene paid attention to them.

Her meaty thighs were parted, and Gene was inside her, pressing between her plump labia folds and slow pumping her. He wasn't far inside her, though, and was being quite careful with the heavy-set woman who was more than three times his age and who controlled his purse strings. He was able to stay hard while fucking her not only because he was young, at twenty-two, and highly sexed, but also by thinking of other lovers entirely while he was fucking her.

He wasn't working on bringing her to climax. He'd already done that. She'd been in the same position, bent over the bed, her arms raised over her head, her fingers rhythmically clawing at the bedspread as, crouched down behind her, in reverse, he'd had his head between her thighs. He'd worked her clit with his tongue and teeth and the folds of her labia and her cunt entrance with his tongue and the fingers of one hand while he stroked her flanks with the other hand. She had moaned deeply for him, shuddered, and then come for him—and then again and again, the climaxes rolling over her as he continued, relentlessly, to work her clit and cunt.

This act, the vaginal penetration, was for Helene too, but not to make her climax. She wanted to feel the power of making the young stud climax as well. The vaginal fuck was to assure herself that she could still make a man hard and come inside her.

Gene moved his right hand out from underneath her torso and brushed her artificially colored black, wavy hair up and away from the back of her neck. He dipped his lips to her neck and kissed her, his hips still swaying back and forth, fucking her at about half his length. She sighed and whispered his name. She also wiggled her buttocks slightly, signaling she was tiring and wanted him to release inside her. Helene took a man's ejaculation inside her as a self-perceived testament to her continued sensual appeal. Sensual appeal was important to Helene. Helene Havlos headed the House of Havlos, a major fashion and fragrance empire. Her world was built on sexual appeal.

Gene Worth was one of the house male models. He also was Helene's live-in boy toy.

He gave her the ejaculation she wanted, giving her another inch and groaning his release, all along imagining an entirely different partner exploding with him. He kissed her on the neck again, and she sighed. Then he patted her on her ample rump, rose off her, and padded off to his adjoining hotel room to shower and dress.

Helene turned her head and watched him walk away before she too went to her own shower. He was a beautiful young man—blond and trim of figure with enough muscling to escape being considered effeminate even though he moved like a dancer. It was his pale-blue eyes and the sunshine of his blond, nearly shoulder-length hair that arrested one's attention first, but it was the sunshine of his smile and his open, welcoming manner that gripped you. Helene, whose family was Greek, always thought of him as a young, lithe Alexander the Greek and continually envisioned him wearing a gold-leaf breast plate, sandals, with straps snaking up his shapely calves—and not much else. She had closed a fashion show with him dressed like this once, and it had made that day's sales soar. She sighed at the sight of his plump, yet firm buttocks swaying slightly as he walked away from her.

Gene hadn't come into Helene's house and bed because of the allure of Helene, whether physical, financial, or a matter of ambition, although she would have said otherwise and had genuinely thought she was correct. He had done so because of her husband, now deceased, Victor Macek. Gene had been working for the House of Havlos before he met the couple and Helene had been vaguely— and favorably—aware of him before. But they had come together at a faculty-student cocktail party at Columbia University in New York City because Gene, as well as modeling and doing a bit of porn for his then-roommate, was studying creative writing at Columbia at night. Victor Macek, a political novelist and Serbian nationalist, who had been chased out of Eastern Europe and was teaching at Columbia, was, coincidentally, not only one of Gene's professors and Helene Havlos's husband, but also was gay and had seen Gene—under the stage name of Will Belayed—in a few of the porn films Gene had done.

Macek had already laid Gene regularly in a New York hotel outside of class before they chanced upon each other at the cocktail party. Helene had taken a shine to Gene and expressed as much to her husband of convenience and, in order to have Gene closer to home himself, unknown to Helene, Macek had proposed that Gene move in with them as an "assistant" to Macek in his writing. Gene, who wanted to write about Macek, the Serbian freedom fighter, had agreed.

Gene moved in, started his research of Macek's past, fucked Helene upon request, was, in turn, fucked by Macek, and benefited by having no housing and few food costs. It was all an adventure that Gene was contemplating using for an eventual novel of his own.

Months later, Macek had been shot dead by Helene's French-accepted hairdresser, who was discovered to actually be Ukrainian, and who immediately turned the gun on himself and was found slumped dead over the body of Macek. The newspapers had immediately latched on the hairdresser's political activist past as a motive for the Moscow-sponsored "assassination" of the Serbian nationalist novelist. Although being the only ones alive who knew that the hairdresser had shot Macek from sexual jealousy rather than romantic and intriguing political motives—he had found Macek in bed with Gene, a bed Macek usually occupied with the hairdresser—Helene and Gene had made a pact of misdirection: Gene had his first *New York Times* feature, a "the Serbian nationalist I knew" piece, under his belt; and the House of Havlos had added yet another intriguing legend to its history. Gene had found his taste of intrigue and adventure quite satisfying—and sexually arousing.

The two were now in New Orleans for an extravaganza of fashion house runway showings at the Marriott convention center in the French Quarter.

When Gene entered Helene's suite again, she was sitting at the vanity in her bathroom, laboriously applying the makeup to her face that took twenty years off her age, a chore she kept at even though her catty detractors said that taking two decades off the mid-seventies was hardly worth the effort. He came in behind her, leaned his chin on her shoulder to give her a dutiful sunshine smile in the mirror on the wall above the vanity desk, slipped his hands into her robe, and cupped her bare breasts. He knew working her breasts was the favorite attention he could give her. She looked at him in the mirror, gave a moan and a sigh, and smiled at him.

"You are so good to me," she murmured.

"You are better to me," he answered. They both were fully aware of what he did for her and why.

"Are you sure you can manage on your own today?" she asked. "I'm sure that even New Orleans is dead on a Sunday morning."

"I'll be fine," he answered. "Maybe I'll just walk around and take the atmosphere in. I'll stay out of trouble." He had no intention of doing much of the former and the latter was an intended lie. He had a taste for adventure and danger. Macek had brought that out in him. The hunky Serb had shown him higher levels of arousal than having dipped into the porn films had.

Gene's stint on the walkway at the fashion show had been the previous day. Only a small portion of the weekend had been allotted to men's fashion. They had talked briefly about him sitting with Helene during today's events, but they had both dismissed that possibilities during the runway events for reasons of their own. As much as Helene liked the thought of showing off her boy toy, she was even more sensitive to how his beauty diminished and aged whatever claim she still had to that. On Gene's part, contrary to the impression he'd given her, he had developed very explicit plans for today. Excepted from this was the gala dinner that evening in the hotel's ballroom.

"You're sure," she said, as she stood at the door, decked out in the height of fashion and looking pretty good for a hefty Eastern European woman of seventy-five.

"Yes, I'm sure," Gene answered with a sigh of resignation as if he faced a day of boredom without her.

"You'll remember to be back in plenty of time for the gala tonight?" she asked as she opened the door.

"Yes, I promised."

"You brought the tux from the house's spring collection?"

"Yes, of course." Above all else, Gene was there to serve and show off the House of Havlos. There wasn't the least bit of misunderstanding about that.

* * * *

Gene didn't meander when he left the hotel. He walked, swiftly, across the French Quarter, northeast on Decatur, to the other side, to Baracks Street, running northwest from the Mississippi River, one street shy of Esplanade Avenue, the boundary between the Quarter and the warehouse area of the Faubourg Marginy district. He understood, just during this walk, what Helene had meant by Sunday morning not being the best time to be exploring the French Quarter. He could tell from the party debris on the streets, the drunks sprawled in the alleys, and the absence of life otherwise that New Orleans had barely gotten to bed and didn't intend to come out again on the day given over to the Lord.

He wasn't here to sightsee, although Decatur did cross over the top of Jackson Square, the heart of the Quarter as well as the city, and he slowed down here. But then he hurried on, repeating in his mind the information he had of his destination—a door just inside an alley off Baracks Street with a neon sign saying "Phillippe's" over it, but you had to look carefully to find it. He'd been assured it would be open and serving even on a Sunday morning—if you didn't arrive much before noon—but as Gene walked the nearly deserted, confetti-infested streets he lost a bit of confidence in what he'd been told.

But he'd been told true. He did look carefully when he turned left from Decatur onto Baracks and there, sure enough, was a doorway just inside an alley entrance with a lit sign of "Phillippe's" over it. He entered the doorway, nodding to the doorkeeper sitting on a stool just inside the door, turned to the right in the darkened space, and followed the rising cloud of smoke and the sound of a saxophone and a husky voice singing in the style of Ella Fitzgerald down a set of stairs and then, turning left, into the club room.

The room wasn't large, and the crowd—some thirty men, sitting one or two to a small table—made it appear even smaller. The atmosphere was dark and smoky; the lights were directed at a platform in front of a small wood dance floor. The platform supported a black baby grand, with a hefty, sweating black piano player; an unoccupied drum set; a saxophonist perched on a wood stool; and a zaftig Hispanic singer in a puffy black wig, a sparkly red-sequined dress with a plunging neckline, and a husky voice that was satisfying and could almost convince you that the vocalist was female, although he wasn't. Two couples, all four of them men—indeed all of the patrons were men—were on the dance floor, partner in close clutches with partner, swaying against each other so intimately that, if they hadn't been clothed, they would have been having sex.

A young waiter—he and Gene probably being the youngest men in the room—guided Gene to a table just inside the edge of the area covered by the light of the spots and smiled at him. He glided off before Gene could order a drink, but within two minutes the waiter was back with two drinks, a beer in a glass mug, and scotch in a glass. Gene looked up quizzically at the waiter.

"The beer is compliments of the man over there," he said, pointing to a middle-aged white man in an expensively cut suit that almost hid his fifteen pounds too much. "And the other drink is from the divine man over there. Lucky you, doll, you got your pick between money and a wild ride." The waiter wafted off and Gene turned his head to see who had sent him the glass of scotch.

It wasn't really a contest unless Gene had come here for a good meal at a steak house rather than to get laid. But he came here to get laid. He smiled, stood, picked up the scotch glass, and moved to the table of the hunk.

And a hunk he was. He looked vaguely familiar, but Gene couldn't place him. He could have been a male model, though, as Gene was—one well into his career, though. He appeared to be at least thirty. He was dark-skinned, but his features had a European cut to them. Wavy black hair, flashing dark eyes, a self-confident smile. What kept his face from perfect was that his nose was slightly broken, which gave him a hint of thugishness, danger, and mystery. His body—or the torso Gene could see—was perfect, though. He was muscular, strained the silkiness of his sport shirt, open three buttons down, revealing that his torso, as was one arm, was heavily tattooed in colorful swirls of some unrecognizable pattern. A gold medallion on a gold chain nestled between his beefy pecs. Gene's first impression was "gorgeous South American drug lord," but that didn't deter Gene. He was slumming, his need for a man having built up for the last two weeks.

"Would you have preferred bourbon?" the man asked when Gene reached the side of the table. "Sit, please. Do you want something else?" The English was American, but there was a hint of something there—something foreign, something that went with the South American impression.

"No, thanks. This is perfect."

"So are you," the man said. "Sit with me. I'm lonely."

"We can't have that," Gene answered and sat—in the chair beside and close to the man rather than across from him. The man put one arm around Gene's shoulder along the top of his seat back and his other hand on Gene's thigh, above his knee. Gene had come down on the chair with his legs together, but when the hand went on his leg, he instinctively widened his stance. That wasn't lost on the man.

"I'm Nick," he said, the voice booming out a bit because the music had just stopped and the small band was taking a break. "Sorry, I'm called Nick," he repeated in a lower voice. "I'm visiting New Orleans. Looking for a bit of company."

"Me too," Gene answered. "I'm Will."

"Will," Nick said, and smiled. Then he gave a little laugh.

"That's funny?" Gene asked. He took a taste of his scotch. The man had ordered the good stuff. He felt a little tingly, as Nick was touching him on the side of his neck with the tips of his fingers and the hand on his thigh had moved to the inside, applying a bit of pressure that caused Gene to widen his stance. Gene also felt himself going hard. He wanted Nick to discover that—with his hand.

"Nothing really. It just when you said you were Will, my thought was 'Will he?'"

"Do you top?" Gene asked, deciding there was no reason not to be direct. He was sure they both knew what had drawn them to this club and he already was thinking of this stud being on top of him, inside him. He already was sure the chocolate-skinned hunk was a bull. I wonder what he'd say if I told him that my porn film name was Will Belayed, he thought, and then laughed himself.

Nick laughed again, no doubt thinking Gene had done so at seeing the surprise in Nick's face.

"Yes, of course I'm a top," he answered. One of Gene's hands reached over and settled on Nick's basket. Nick gave another little laugh at Gene's reaction when he found that the man was hard and was, indeed, a bull. Nick's hand glided up the inside of Gene's thigh, found the line of Gene's cock, dressed right, and settled there. They didn't speak for a long minute as they felt each other up. Nick was the first to break, his hand came back up to the surface of table. He picked up his glass, drained it, and caught the attention of the passing waiter.

"You want another one?" he turned and asked Gene. Then he had to repeat himself because Gene had been sprawled out on his chair, legs parted, buttocks on the edge, a dreamy look on his face from the work Nick had been doing on his cock through the material of his linen trousers.

"Uh, no thanks. I haven't finished this one," he said, snapping back to the present. He took a long pull at the drink, though, which indicated it wouldn't be long before it was finished.

"Two more of the same," Nick said to the waiter, who registered the order and drifted away. "Are we going to fuck?" he asked Gene in a calm, straightforward voice.

"I think so. But you don't have to get me drunk to get me in bed," Gene answered.

"Good to know. You play squash? You look like you're in good shape. But not like you're into rough work."

"I model. I have to keep in shape for that. But I'm also going to school and I do some writing—that's what I'm training to do."

"Not high school I hope."

"No. Graduate school at Columbia."

"Columbia, as in New York City?"

"Yes."

"I'm from New York too. You are small and look young. Had to ask about the school."

"I understand. The size goes with the modeling."

"That's fine. Your body's perfect. Well, your hips look really slim. I hope—"

"That won't be a problem."

"Because I'm—"

"Big. Yes, I know."

The drinks arrived and the two men looked away from each other, suddenly showing interest in the crowd around them. The band had returned and was starting into another tune.

"Yes, I play squash," Gene said, retreating from the direction the conversation had quickly taken.

"Do you dance?"

"Yes."

"Then let's dance," Nick said. They rose from the table and moved toward the floor. On his feet, Nick was no less the muscular hunk he looked on a chair behind a table, but there was one pronounced distinction. He limped pronounceably as he moved to the dance floor. Once there, though, the limp wasn't noticeable. Once in his clutches on the dance floor, Gene could only think about how sensual a dancer Nick was—and how commanding. And sexy. They swayed against each other to the crooning slow jazz tone the drag queen was singing on the stage. Eyes were rivetted to them, the men in the room realizing they weren't just dancing; they were dry fucking.

Nick had moved a hand between them, unzipped himself, and taken his cock out. He had pulled Gene up and set him down, with the long, thick, hard cock penetrating between the younger man's thighs below his ball sack, and they were swaying against each other, Nick's dick moving in and out between Gene's thighs, dry fucking as they moved to the slow, sensual rhythm of the music. Nick was taller and bulkier than Gene, so the younger man, Nick having pulled him up to where he couldn't reach the floor with his feet, had one leg wrapped around Nick's thigh and the other one just hanging. Panting heavily, he let his arms dangle and Nick held him up with an arm around his waist.

Those watching them knew they were dry fucking. They would have been fine if the two had stripped and fucked in the raw, and the tables where there were couples had some humping going on as well. Gene would have been fine with that too, but Nick showed that he was in control—and that he wasn't ready for it yet.

They kissed and as they came out of the kiss, Gene murmured, "Take me someplace. Take me someplace and fuck my lights out. Is there—?"

"Yes, I have a room. But I have rituals. I'm athletic. I have to blow off some steam first; work you up to begging for it. Were you shitting me about knowing how to play squash?"

"Yes, I play squash," Gene answered.

As they walked out of the club, passing by the table only long enough for Nick to drop enough money to cover drinks, including the last round that had been delivered but not consumed, and a tip, Gene saw it again—the pronounced limp of Nick, which seemed incongruous as much in shape and as young as the man was.

Such a man of mystery, Gene thought. And before too long he's going to be on top of me, inside of me, fucking me with that big cock of his. He shivered in pleasure and anticipation.

They passed the table of the middle-aged money man who had sent Gene a beer. He looked up and smiled at Gene but there was no animosity in his face. A young man was sitting with him, close, and had a hand between the money man's legs. The young man looked like a pro. Money man obviously was going to get what he wanted when he'd come to Phillippe's.

On impulse, Gene leaned over and whispered, "No offense meant. Thanks for the beer."

"You didn't drink the beer," the man said, his voice and eyes showing uncertainty, like he wondered if Gene was putting him on, taunting him. To be clear, though, Gene took the man's hand and placed it on his basket, letting the man cop a feel of a cock Nick had made hard. He leaned further down and kissed the man on the lips. "It's the gesture that counts. It's Sunday, I would have gone with you and I would have been happy to give you a good time."

Then he turned and caught up with Nick at the door, leaving the man smiling and turning back to the other young man with greater confidence.

"Are you always that easy?" Nick asked in amusement.

"Only on Sunday," Gene answered. "And on Sunday you can do anything you want with me," he added. "I'm pretty straight laced the other days of the week."

"Remember you said that," Nick murmured.

* * * *

Nick showed that he, indeed, was athletic. Not only that; he showed that having a bum leg didn't slow him down much at all. Gene was a good squash player too, fast, lithe, and flexible. He was always there, ready to flick the ball into the most difficult to return position. Nick was up to the challenge, though, impressing Gene from the start by putting a rubber ball with a yellow dot—the mark of an advanced player—into play. Where Gene shone in dexterity and reflexes, Nick won out in drive and strategy, He dominated the T just as Gene instinctively knew the older, more muscular man would dominate him. He wore Gene down and conquered him in the game just as Gene was looking forward to having it play out in bed.

Gene had thought being taken to Claude's Gym and Spa on Mandeville Street in the nearby Faubourg Marginy section was a bit weird, but he had to admit that the squash match with Nick had him panting for the man. This was an experienced athlete. There must, Gene thought, be a story behind the limp that was connected with athletics—probably professional athletics.

The match had keyed Gene up sexually. Nick had his sports bag with him and pulled out two jocks and skimpy shorts and the two played "skins," which gave them plenty of opportunity to build up a heat for each other. It almost was as if he knew this was where he'd be bringing whoever he picked up at Phillippe's. And even though he'd said he was visiting from New York City as well, he had known this gym was here—and that it was a hangout for gay guys—and only gay guys.

And he knew it had an action sauna. The sauna, after a sweaty squash game and a quick cold shower, was where the action started in earnest for the two men who were panting for each other by the time they entered the sauna. Gene stretched out on his back, a towel across his lap, on an upper bench, and Nick, naked and sitting on his towel, sat on the level below him. Nick was all muscular and colorful tattoo, with chocolate background, male beauty. The thickness and bent-over-from heaviness long cock of his that was half hard when he entered the sauna had drawn the attention of all the men and made them gasp—Gene no less than the others. He could appreciate why Nick might wonder if his narrow hips might portend a channel unable to accommodate it.

They didn't anal fuck in the sauna, but they put on quite a show regardless.

"Turn over," Nick had commanded, and Gene turned onto his belly, ready for Nick to mount him there and then and fuck him. Gene was fairly moaning for it.

"Yes, yes, fuck me," he whined.

But Nick didn't fuck him. He straddled his buttocks, pushed Gene's towel off him, and rested the underside of his cock in Gene's crack like he was preparing to fuck him, but, instead, he massaged Gene's back, while the young man moaned. Other men gathered in the sauna, watching, and stroking themselves, and, as the show progressed, stroked each other.

"Turn on your back," Nick directed, moving back down to the level below Gene. Gene did as commanded, with a groan. Nick knelt below him, leaned over, and took Gene's mouth in his in a kiss. He fisted Gene's cock and stroked him off. Gene reached down and sheathed Nick's cock in his hand and stroked him as well. The kissing and stroking continued as other men in the sauna watched and groaned.

Gene came first, with a shudder and a jerk of his body. Nick grasped Gene's leg toward the front of the bench and folded the young man's knee up into Gene's body. "Keep it there," he growled. His right hand glided up the other thigh and one of his fingers penetrated Gene's passage. Gene groaned and arched his back. Nick came up on his knees, his long dick in line with Gene's mouth, and Nick finger-fucked Gene's passage with first one finger, and eventually, four at once, up to the knuckles.

The other men in the sauna who were watching and who Nick made sure could see his fingers penetrate Gene's ass groaned as well.

"Good, very good," Nick murmured. "You could take two."

Gene turned his head, took Nick's cock in his mouth, and sucked the older man to a facial ejaculation. Gene's left hand had been busy stroking himself off again, and he came a second time shortly after Nick did.

The other men in the sauna were vocal about the two continuing and agreed that they wanted to watch Nick fuck Gene, but Nick vetoed that and the two went off to the showers again.

Nick did fuck Gene, over a period of more than two hours, and in several demanding positions, but that was at the room he'd rented for the day at a B&B on the nearby Burgundy Street.

Gene did have difficulty taking all of Nick's cock— at least for the first fuck—but he was determined to do it and wanted it all inside him—and that's what he got. After reaming his passage to the needs of his thick cock, Nick tested it further, spreading the entrance with his fingers and penetrating with his cock without removing the fingers, and, ultimately, working Gene with both his cock and a dildo simultaneously. Gene managed it all, each time welcoming the pain-pleasure of the fuck. It was with great reluctance that he decided it was too late for another go at it late in the afternoon.

"I have to go, I'm afraid. I have someplace to be tonight."

"Me too," Nick said, as he dried his hair with a towel, coming out of the attached bath, naked.

Gene shuddered. The man was gorgeous and he'd been magnificent in bed. Gene had never been as hard or had been filled and worked that well—or had come that frequently.

"I guess that's it for us, then," he said. "I'll be leaving tomorrow."

"Me too," Nick said. Gene lay there, hoping that the man would be the one to say they both lived in New York, so maybe . . . possibly . . . probably, he hoped, they could just get it on again there. But Nick didn't say it, so maybe Gene was just a one-time lay for him. Maybe he wasn't impressed with Gene enough to meet him in New York. And Nick thought he was named Will. He wouldn't have a way to track him down. They hadn't exchanged last names even.

There was nothing about today, Sunday in New Orleans, that had more than a one-day hookup vibe to it—other than that Gene melted to this chocolate god with the South American accent.

Apparently it wasn't the same for Nick who, after he was dressed, said, "No worry about the hotel bill. I prepaid. You were a great lay. Thanks." And then he was gone.

* * * *

"What a marvelous day that was. Our line stood up very well. I was sure Oscar Oliphant was bringing something special this year and he does seem to have found a second wind, but all of our spies came back with comments that spoke of us favorably against this line. Have you showered yet? Yes, I think that tux shirt goes better than the other one you brought. You'll look divine. We'll both be perfect. I'll be soaking in the tub. Anyone calls, just take the messages—unless it's Oscar. He said he wanted to talk with me about something."

Helene had begun her monologue as she entered the suite. Gene hadn't beaten her back to the hotel and up to the rooms by more time than it had taken him to shower and start pulling his tux accessories out of the tissue paper before she had twirled into the room, clearly on cloud nine from the success of her part of the day's runway event.

She hadn't asked him about his day. All the way back across the French Quarter to the Marriott, the streets still Sunday subdued, he'd worked on being about to produce a plausible and benign report on what he'd done that day. He could say he'd gone to the jazz club. Telling her he'd gone to a gym or played squash would raise more questions than it would satisfy, though. His Sunday in New Orleans hadn't been dull, but it wasn't anything he could tell her about. And he truly liked Helene; it wasn't all because she paid for him. But she'd returned all wrapped up in herself and her own day. He hadn't had to explain a thing.

She lit up as soon as they entered the ballroom and she looked at her invitation card and then over to their assigned table. "He's there. They have us sitting with Oscar Oliphant. And who is that divine man with him?"

Who indeed? Gene thought. Standing with Oliphant, heavenly decked out in a tuxedo, stood Nick. Gene did a doubletake. It occurred to him then, though, that Nick didn't seem a bit surprised—just amused.

"Oscar, it looks like they have us seated together this evening," Helene said as they approached the table. She was all bubbly. Oliphant was a handsome man. He was in his fifties, but he'd taken good care of himself. He was tall and slim and, naturally, elegantly and expensively dressed. Everything was cut close, sexy, though, and Gene was able even to discern the line of his left-dressed cock, which was long and thick. His salt-and-pepper hair was wavy and the material of his dress shirt was so thin that Gene could see the pattern of his chest hair and the puffiness of his nipples. He wondered if Helene saw him as such or whether Nick had Gene so tight up with sexual thoughts that he was seeing more in the dress designer than was there.

Oliphant was eyeing him with great interest.

"I'm glad they have put us together," he was saying. He was speaking to Helene but looking at Gene. "I have the request I said I wanted to make of you. We can discuss it."

"This is one of my models, Gene Worth," Helene said in introducing Gene.

"And this is the manager of my models, Ricardo Faria," Oliphant said, introducing the man Gene had been told was named Nick. And now, hearing that name, it clicked. Ricardo Faria had been a star soccer player for Brazil. But a leg injury had knocked him out of professional football. It all clicked into place, including Nick—Ricardo—not being surprised to see him here. As the head of Oliphant's models, Faria would know the models of the other New York houses. And he didn't have to propose they could meet in New York. Faria apparently knew where to find him in New York. Gene thought back to who had told him about the jazz club, Phillippe's. As he remembered it had been one of the fashion photographers—someone who worked with Oliphant's house as well as Helene's. Oliphant confirmed that the softening-up encounter with Faria quite possibly had been a setup, as he continued to speak to Helene.

"I have a small male line coming out in a few weeks and I know your male line season is over now. I need a few models. Ricardo has been going through the books, and he thinks your Mr. Worth here is just who we need. Do you think—?"

"We certainly could discuss it," Helene said. "It would depend, of course, on what Gene would like to do. He has studies too. He's in a graduate writing program at Columbia."

"Is he?" Faria asked, with a smile. "How interesting."

Gene wanted to belt him one for the amused smile.

"Perhaps we could borrow him for a couple of hours after the banquet to tell him what is involved," Oliphant said, as he pulled a chair out for Helene to sit in.

"Perhaps, if he wants to," she said as she sank her bulk into the chair.

As she did so, Oliphant turned to Gene. Faria was standing behind Gene with his hands holding Gene's hips possessively.

"I understand you go by the name Will in some situations," the designer murmured to Gene, his eyes sparkling with the smile.

"Sometimes," Gene responded.

"Will you . . . for me?" Oliphant asked, reaching out in a way that they could not be observed and stroking Gene's basket with long, slender fingers.

Gene showed that he "will," that he would, and that he did.

The three of them were standing, naked on the carpet in the center of Oscar Oliphant's suite at the Marriott New Orleans. Gene was bent over at the waist, grasping his ankles with his hands. Ricardo was behind him, hands grasping the young model's waist, his cock slowly plowing Gene's ass. Oliphant was standing in front of Gene.

Oliphant ran the long, slender fingers of one hand into Gene's hair, gripped his hair, and lifted his head up, bringing Gene's mouth into position to open to his cock. After a few minutes of working Gene this way, Oliphant waved a bottle of poppers under Gene's nose a couple of times and pulled his dick out of Gene's mouth. He leaned down and kissed Gene on the mouth. Ricardo continued pumping him from behind.

Dropping the bottle of poppers on the carpet, Oliphant signaled to Ricardo, who leaned back, arching Gene's body back with him. He reached down and gripped Gene's thighs and raised and spread them. Oliphant moved in between Gene's spread legs, positioned his cock head at Gene's passage entrance above the root of Ricardo's already-buried cock, and started to work his cock in above Ricardo's. Gene moaned and groaned at the testing, but he took them both. He now knew why the man he'd known as Nick had wanted to test his channel with his cock and a dildo together earlier in the day.

Across the room, a grandfather's clock struck the half hour. It was 11:30 p.m.—still Sunday New Orleans.

Chapter Three: Chicago Sunday

A tower bell of a church somewhere beyond the hotel on Chicago's North Side was peeling off the call to a service, and it seemed that Ricardo was coordinating his thrusts with the bell tolling. The hunky Brazilian was on top of Gene, doing him in a missionary, on the king-sized bed in Oscar Oliphant's sixth-floor Armitage Hotel room. He was hovering over the younger male model, his knees between Gene's bent legs, his hands pressing the young man's upper arms to the mattress, his face close enough to Gene's, a look of determination in his eyes, that his loose shoulder-length black hair was tickling Gene's throat and the tops of his bare shoulders as it moved with the hard, big-cock thrusts of his pelvis. Ricardo was intent on getting every bit of pleasure from the friction of his thrusts inside the young model that he could get before releasing his seed.

With a moan, Gene raised his buttocks from the mattress, giving the Brazilian deeper access, which the man took advantage of, thrust a few more time, tightened and jerked, filled the bulb of his condom, and rolled off to the right of Gene, onto his back. He was snoring within a minute. But he had a contented smile on his face. Gene was one of the best lays he'd ever had.

Gene wasn't finished with his servicing responsibilities, though. Oscar Oliphant had been lying on his side to the left of Gene, facing him, stroking Gene's cock with his hand while Ricardo fucked Gene. Oscar had had first fuck with Gene, taking him in a straightforward missionary, with Ricardo sitting on the side of the bed and helping to guide the thrusts with a hand on Oscar's bare buttocks. Having shot his load, Oscar had rolled off to the side of the bed, while Ricardo moved over on top of Gene for his turn.

While Ricardo took over the fuck and Oscar was stroking Gene's cock with one hand, the fashion designer had a marijuana joint in his other hand and was puffing on that. He loosened the hold of his hand and Gene kept moving his hips, fucking up into the loose sheath of Oscar's folded fingers until, with a sigh, he came. Oscar moved the joint to Gene's mouth, and the young man took a couple of puffs before, his mind becoming clouded, he brushed it away, crawled out from between the two men, and went to the hotel room window.

He could see the church bell tower beyond a park, on West Webster Avenue, which would dead end in three blocks into Lakeshore Park fronting on Lake Michigan. They weren't in a high-rise part of the city, but they weren't far from the city center. The hotel was a bit seedy and off the beaten path, but that was natural for a building with a gentleman's club, the Stag Club, on the eighth, top, floor and a bar of ill repute on the ground floor. They were in town to peddle one of the House of Oliphant's men's fashion lines to retailers. Gene and another male model, Chip, were there to model the clothing, much of it sexy wear for adult boutiques and gay male online retailers, in a fashion show this afternoon in the Stag Club. Ricardo Faria, once a star soccer player in Brazil who had been sidelined by a leg injury, was there to keep Gene and Chip under control and in line.

Gene had been with the House of Oliphant for nearly six months. Before that he was with the House of Havlos and was being shared between the fashion house's maven, Helene, and her Serbian nationalist husband Victor Macek. Gene had been with Victor when the man had been blown away by Helene's jealous hairdresser. Although both Helene and Gene continued with their arrangement for several months, the specter of Victor, who Gene had been taking writing classes from at Columbia University and who was the model for a Yugoslavia freedom fighter in the novel Gene was writing, remained in both their minds. When Ricardo seduced Gene and Oscar wanted Gene to model for his fashion house, Gene made the move to Oscar's fashion house. The move still rankled a bit, both because Ricardo had been duplicitous in seducing Gene and Gene had seen money exchange hands in the change of his modeling contract. He couldn't help feeling a whore in multiple dimensions. That Oscar and Ricardo regularly shared Gene in a threesome, sometimes doubling him by both being inside him at once, only drove home this feeling.

He could clearly see the park—Oz Park—from here, and he ached for the freedom to be there, to walk free, and, if he fell into a hookup, this being Sunday, a day he felt wanton, it would be one of his own choice. He'd been told he wouldn't only be modeling on this trip—that some of the more important retailers coming to the fashion show expected accommodation by the models. He had complained to Ricardo, who had laughed and said, "You and Chip will be taking care of the tops. I've got to service the bottoms myself. Don't complain to me."

Oscar joined Gene at the window, coming in behind him and holding him close. They both were naked, and Oscar, an older man, but slim and hard of body and elegant of manner, was in erection, his already-sheathed cock pressing at the small of Gene's back. He reached around Gene with both hands. One palmed Gene's sternum and the other offered the joint to Gene again. The young man took a couple of puffs. Oscar took another puff himself and then placed the joint in an ash tray on top of the bureau next to the window. That hand now went to Gene's chin, pulling Gene's head back toward into his chest. His other palm glided down Gene's torso to his belly, and gently pulled back.

"Present to me," Oscar whispered.

With a sigh, Gene changed his position, widening the stance of his legs, pushing his buttocks back and raising them, and pressing the palms of his hands on the window. His eyes watered briefly and he yawned his mouth open at the penetration of the cock, but he gave no sound other than beginning to pant and his breath going ragged as Oscar forced his cock up into the young man's passage deep and began the rhythm of the fuck.

Gene stared out into space, fixating on the park beyond the next block—Oz Park—thinking of being there, free to do as he liked—to pick up men of his own choice. Oscar's attentions were getting to him, though. He took men's cocks not just because he needed the money. He took men's cocks because he enjoyed being shafted— especially on Sundays. And Oscar had a very nice cock and an expert fuck technique. He made love to every inch of Gene's channel. Gene took both Oscar's and Ricardo's cocks together because it was a sense of pride that he could and it was a sense of power that two such beautiful men could have such passion for him at the same time.

He sighed and began moving his pelvis with the deep, slow thrusts. He didn't want to be this easy, but he couldn't help it.

"Yes, yes, right there, like that," he murmured. "Yes, fuck me. Like that."

Ricardo Faria give out a snort in his sleep from across the room. Oscar contributed a little laugh and continued moving his hips as Gene sighed. In, out, in deeper, hold . . . sigh . . . out . . . in . . .

The church bell had started chiming again. Oscar's thrusts were right on the beat. He had moved his hand to Gene's cock and was stroking him. Oscar had long, elegant fingers and soft hands. On the last strike of the church bell, Gene shot his cloudy load against the lower panel of the window, watching the glob dribble down the glass, as Oscar's cum, the fashion designer having pulled out and stripped off the condom before ejaculating, dribble down Gene's inner thigh.

Oscar pulled away from Gene and headed toward the bathroom and the showers, while Ricardo came over, took Gene in an embrace, kissed him on the lips, and led him back to the bed, where, bending the young man over the mattress and forcing Gene's arms over his head with a firm grasp on both of his wrists, Ricardo mounted him and began the dance of the fuck one more time.

* * * *

Gene sat at the desk in his third-floor hotel room, going over a chapter of his novel draft. He was taking the manuscript with him everywhere he went these days and whenever he had a few minutes to spare, he worked on it. It was his escape from his nearly sex slave existence in the world of fashion, albeit how submissively and willingly he acquiesced to it. The novel almost was just the way he wanted it, and his mind kept going to what he could use as an escape after it was done. He always could write about the reality of a male model in the fashion world, but that wouldn't provide him an escape from this world, a world of pleasure, yes, but of almost unbearable intensity and lack of control. Thus, he kept tinkering with the book he had. He knew that the danger at this point was to overmassage it, to suck all of his own voice out of it. He barely touched it these days without the thought of "First do no harm."

The knock at the door jolted him out of the fantasy world he was in—and the memories of Victor Macek—when he had his nose in the manuscript.

"We should be up there already." Chip was at the door. "It will start in fifteen and we need to be ready to walk off the first ensemble."

"I'm already dressed, Chip," Gene answer. "Go ahead. I'll be right behind you."

65

He, in fact, *was* already dressed—in black. The first pass on the catwalk would be making an all-black, dangerous leather statement. He was wearing a mesh muscle athletic T-shirt over tight black leather jeans, with a drop codpiece at the crotch. Black boots. The hand whip was already set up in the Stag Club, behind the stage. He had a black beret to put on too. He had to remember to swagger down the catwalk in this. The clothes were tight, sexy. It was the most coverage of his body that there would be on him for this show. The buyers were looking for sexy—and easily removed. This wasn't the usual set of buyers—these men, mainly men, mainly men who wanted other men—were buying for gay sex clubs and online catalogs.

Gene came out first. Chip, a little older than he was and darker and more pouty and more muscular, followed on the catwalk behind him in the same black leather jeans but bare-chested with a black leather harness. He was wearing black leather gloves and also carried—and swished as he strutted—the hand whip.

The room was long and narrow, like the one at Punto, in New York, that Helene often used for House of Havlos fashion shows. But it was a smaller room than Punto's catwalk room was. The crowd was smaller too, but it looked like a lot of people from Gene's position on the catwalk as he took the long walk down and then off to the slightly wider raised platform at either side at the end, where he went one direction and Chip the other and where both did their turns to the snapping of the cameras before returning to the backstage for the quick change down into something ever skimpier as they moved toward the end of the show.

Most of the patrons were men, although there were some hard-looking women too, who ate the models up with their eyes as much as any of the men did. Gene had encountered some of them before—women who reveled in getting a gay boy hard, of coaxing him inside her, and then snapping her steel trap of a cunt shut and milking him as he screamed at the brutality of her taking. He'd made the mistake of going with one of these women after a show like this, a woman who proved she was stronger and more experienced than he was and who held him captive in position, as she milked him again and again, until his balls ached and he cried out for a mercy she didn't grant him.

Luckily, there would be none of those staying on after the show for the after-event special treatment given to the high rollers who wanted to stay and who were good for big orders of the clothing. At the end, Gene and Chip were down to lacy panties only, with slits in front and back and opaque pouches that clearly revealed what they were packing.

Four men, three middle-aged, hefty, and no beauties, and one highly acceptable one, remained when the crowd cleared and Gene and Chip had been called back out on the catwalk by Oscar Oliphant, standing at the lectern on stage and Ricardo Faria, standing with the four men and refereeing what followed.

Two of the men fucked Gene, with one of the men leaning back into one of the catwalk extensions and pulling Gene's buttocks into his crotch. The better looking of the two athletically crouched, feet on the catwalk, in front of Gene and fed his cock into Gene's mouth. The middle-aged man pulled Gene's passage into his cock through the slit in the back of Gene's panties, raised and spread Gene's legs and fucked him hard. The man remained dressed and Gene was still in his panties. The slit in the back of them, though, gave the man's cock full access to Gene's hole. His cock was thick, the capability of his reach deep. The saving grace for Gene at first was that the man at his head was the best looking of the retailers. He managed to move an arm back under his buttocks and stroke Gene off as he face fucked him and the other man fucked Gene in a doggie. The good-looking guy was in great shape and athletic.

The better-looking of the buyers grew bored with the facing fucking and the tableau moved into double penetration, with the good-looking one hoping off the catwalk, moving to between Gene's legs, and lifting and spreading them more than the man under Gene had done. He entered Gene's passage above the already buried cock and began to stroke. The man was good looking, his kisses were sweet, neither of the men were bulls—and Gene had done this before—so he went with it and took them both, giving them both the good time Ricardo had promised them.

Both Gene and Chip had, of course, known that servicing the key buyers would be part of the show, and both were being appropriately compensated.

The other two men had Chip bent over the seat of one of the guest chairs, with one man doggie fucking him and the other face feeding him.

If any of the retailers availed themselves of Ricardo's cock, Gene didn't see that happen, so he figured that Ricardo had just fed him a line of bull about that rather than sympathy.

The two models escaped back to their separate rooms and their showers and bottles of mouth wash, while Oscar took the clothing orders from the satisfied retailers.

But Gene only thought he had escaped. When he got back to the room, there was a knock at the door.

"My order was extra big," the more presentable of the retailers said when Gene opened the door. "He told me what room you were in and said for you to let me come in."

Dipping his head, Gene took a step back to let the not-so-old, and in-great-shape retailer in the room. They fucked on the bed initially. The retailer was almost tender at first. As Gene had already known, he had a nice cock. And he knew how to use it. Gene sighed for him as the man covered him on the bed and took him half way to heaven in a missionary. For an encore, though, the man challenged Gene's flexibility with "swinging from the chandelier" challenging sex positions that used the whole room and that had Gene groaning deeply and panting hard.

Gene didn't mind all that much. Sunday was his slut day. But he still would like to be making these decisions for himself—and taking any profit there was for them rather than the bulk of that going to Oscar and Ricardo. It turned out, though, that it wasn't that bad. The man cocked him very well, and he left a generous tip on the bureau, both of which Gene marked as profit on Sundays.

* * * *

Gene showered again after the retailer had left his room and sat at the desk and returned to working on his manuscript. He couldn't hold his concentration on that, though. He and the retailer had been in synch in their first fuck. It was the fuck that Gene ached for, while the second, wild fuck was what he generally got. Once the connection had been made that first and the man was inside him and they were rocking their bodies together, Gene had fallen into the rhythm, digging his fingernails into the man's plump buttocks, going with the pattern of the thrusts, and flexing and releasing his fingerholds to the beat of the man inside him, responding to the man whispering in his ear how sweet and tight he was.

The second fuck was much more demanding and vigorous, but the man was an expert. He had brought Gene off three time and he'd left him a tip. Gene couldn't ask for any more—especially on a Sunday.

But then he knew he could ask for more—that he could want more. He could have had control for himself and his body. In this encounter in his room, as with everything else that had happened so far that day, Oscar

Oliphant—backed up by Ricardo Faria—had had control. Even this evening that would happen. Oscar said they'd be eating dinner with the biggest vendor of the House of Oliphant adult men's line of clothing, who had seen photos of Gene and wanted to fuck him. He'd been too important to come to the fashion show, but he was here in Chicago and he wanted to fuck Gene. So, at Oscar's declaration, the four of them, Oscar, Ricardo, Gene, and the retailor, named Harold, would sit down to dinner in the bar on the first floor and at the end of dinner there would only be Gene and Harold. Then there would be this hotel room. Gene was warned that Harold was rough. If that hookup hadn't been planned, Chip and Gene would have been put in the same hotel room.

Gene felt the walls of the room closing in on him. Everywhere he turned, Oscar's control was there. And Oscar had bought him—his contract—from Helene, so Gene felt he was no more than Oscar's trained monkey. And, worse, he, Gene, was weak. Whenever he was ready to blow, Oscar was there, stroking him, gathering him in, fucking him—and once again reminding Gene that he was weak in the face of the constraints and control being applied to him.

He had to get out of here. He had to be somewhere and do something that was of his own choice. He'd brought athletic gear. He exercised every day to stay in model shape. He dressed in a jock strap, athletic shorts and T-shirt, and running shoes, without socks. He grabbed a water bottle and hand towel and slipped out of the hotel. He gave no thought to where he was headed, but he found himself in Oz Park, running the pathways.

Gene nearly exhausted himself in the mindless run on the park's paths. Near the center of the park, he collapsed on a bench, toweled his face and neck off, and took a deep swig of the water. That was better. He was feeling better. He was feeling more in control. He knew it was a false sense of control, but then he thought maybe not, when he noticed that a rangy, gang-looking black guy had passed the bench for the third time, each time turning toward him and giving him "the eye."

He looked like a bad side of Chicago thug. He was tall and thin, wearing baggy shorts, riding low on his narrow waist, with a long silver chain hanging, looped off a heavy leather belt barely holding the shorts up. His athletic T was cut deep at the sides and the neck, showing bulging biceps and pecs and considerable tattooing. He looked mean as hell.

He was just the type of guy Oscar wouldn't want Gene to go with.

On the third pass, the thug stopped, turned, gave Gene a wide smile and a wink and popped his tongue in his cheek. He grabbed his crotch and gave it a shake. He inclined his head toward the opening of a smaller path going deeper in the park's foliage. Then he turned and slowly started walking down that path. This wasn't like the hookups Gene had engaged in in New York's Central Park. This was more primeval, dangerous, raw.

Gene rose from the bench and followed him.

They had reached the fuck stage in the bushes off that path when they froze at the sound of a couple of women, speaking loudly, and an unknown number of squealing children dancing around them moving down the path toward the two men.

Gene was standing, but crouched over, his head pushed toward the soil under the bushes by a strong black hand pressing on the back of his neck. Gene's wrists were bound behind his back with the chain that had been hanging from the black thug's belt. The black guy was folded over Gene's body, his free hand palming Gene's belly. Gene's athletic shorts were puddled around his ankles, as were the black thug's around his. The black guy's cock, possibly the longest Gene had ever taken in his throat before—they were beyond the preliminary now—was inside Gene's ass, moving deeper, as Gene writhed and huffed and puffed through the wadding of his athletic shirt that was stuffed in his mouth.

They weren't just preparing to fuck; they already were fucking.

At the sound of the approaching women and their bevy of urchins, the thug pulled his dick out of Gene, hissed for Gene to follow him further into the foliage, jerked up his shorts, whipped the chain off Gene's wrists, and turned and pulled Gene away with him. Gene, whimpering, barely had time to pull his shorts up before he was being pulled into the bushes.

He was pushed and pulled to a derelict stone building, with a pitted and overgrown pathway leading to it from who knows where. The door was covered by a steel sheet, but the thug had no trouble pushing that aside and pulling Gene into what turned out to be an abandoned restroom.

Gene was pulled into a toilet stall, the door of which had been ripped half off and was leaning open.

They started from the beginning again, the thug pushing Gene down onto his ass on the toilet, grabbing his wrists and forcing his arms over his head, the wrists against the porcelain tiles of the back wall, and feeding his long cock down Gene's throat. Gene gave him good head, which made the thug grunt his satisfaction, withdraw his cock, pull Gene up and around, putting him on his knees. He slammed Gene's head against the back wall a couple of times to hear Gene yelp and then sob and to completely subdue him. He strapped Gene on the back and buttocks a few times with his leather belt for effect, bound his wrists behind his back with the chain again, mounted his ass, and fucked him vigorously and cruelly in a doggie fuck to the thug's ejaculation.

When the black bull had shot his load, Gene realized that he wasn't sheathed, that he had barebacked him and was creaming him deep with multiple plasterings of hot cum. Gene cried out in ecstasy at the total taking.

He was left on the floor of the abandoned restroom, curled up in a fetal position, rocking back and forth, and . . . humming.

It had been exhilarating. It had taken his breath away. The thug had been an expert cocksman and had one of the world's longest cocks. He'd reach into the soft core and jerked climaxes out of Gene such as the young man had never felt before. Gene had been ravished and mastered, fucked dirty and raw, and it had made him feel alive.

And he had chosen it—the choice of being taken brutally like this had been under his control—not Oscar's or Ricardo's or Helene's or the dead Victor's. And Oscar had not benefited in any way from the ravishing of his sex slave.

This was a Sunday to remember.

* * * *

Gene did what he could to hide the superficial wounds he had suffered—if "suffered" was a fair word to be used for what was done to him to soar his arousal into the stratosphere—before he went down to the hotel bar for a drink and a light supper. A long-sleeve shirt, despite the steamy summer temperatures in Chicago, took care of the chain chaff marks on his wrists. He had a diaphanous shirt that highlighted his fine torso but that had thick wrist cuffs. The welts on his back and buttocks were barely noticeable—or so he believed—and they wouldn't show during supper. He'd rubbed a bit of blemish-masking cream on them and would just make sure the lights were low when he took the retailer back to his room.

The cut on his forehead from having his head bounced off the wall behind the toilet was something else. But the bruise would be worse tomorrow than tonight. He had makeup he could use to minimize that. And he could hope the lighting in the bar would be low.

The lighting in the bar area *was* low, the effect of the stage lit up where there was a pianist and singer making it even dimmer where the audience sat, but Oscar was eagle-eyed enough to notice the makeup on his model's forehead and he rose and met Gene at the door of the bar. Marred skin was anathema to a fashion model.

"Whatever happened . . . what did you do this afternoon?" he asked in a hiss.

"I fell. I'm sorry. I don't think my brow is what this john of yours will want to play with," Gene answered. "Is he here yet?"

"Yes, he's here. And don't even joke about calling Mr. Salisbury a john. His first name is Harold. And you are to do for him anything he wants from you."

"Oh, I can see where you wouldn't want to call him a john then," Gene said. His afternoon had made him feisty. Oscar saw the flash in the young man's eyes and bit off what he might have said. He would deal with this later. He put on a fake smile and guided Gene back to the table in a dark corner of the room.

Gene's spirits took a nosedive as they approached the table. The man was a sweaty toad. He seemed nervous at the situation, although anxious to get at Gene too—his eyes lit up when he saw Gene approaching. He was fifty if he was a day and at least 250 pounds. And ugly as sin. He looked disheveled and his suit didn't fit him at all well, which was an unfortunate surprise considering that he was important enough in the clothing distribution industry to command his own whore boy from a fashion designer.

But this was the job. Gene slid in beside him and gave him a sexy smile. He didn't even flinch when a big hand gripped his knee painfully under the table. The introductions went OK until Gene lifted an arm at one point and his sleeve pulled back enough for Oscar to see the burn marks on his wrist. Oscar gave Gene a venomous stare at that point, but luckily the waiter arrived for their drink and dinner orders, and when he was finished and walked away from the table, the pianist and singer had returned from their breaks and started another set.

Gene did what he could to maintain conversation and the required flirting with Harold Salisbury, while the clothing distributor fairly slobbered over him in anticipation of getting him alone. When he could, Gene looked around at the other tables. In doing so, his eyes met with a man across the room who seemed to be as uncomfortable with his dinner companions as Gene was and who showed all of the attributes that Gene would have liked to see in a man he'd been hooked up with to bed him later. The man was probably in his early fifties, just as Salisbury was, but he was trim and handsome in a rugged way, and he wore his tuxedo like he too was a male model. His eyes sparkled when his gaze met Gene's and he had an engaging smile. He was bearded, with salt and pepper hair, but the beard was close cropped and expertly trimmed.

Increasingly, Gene found his attention drifting away from his table to elsewhere in the room. He frequently went back to looking at the gentleman across the room, and when he did, he found the man was watching him. It occurred to him that, from their relative positions, the man could tell that Salisbury had a hand on Gene's thigh under the table—and then his inner thigh, and eventually his basket. The hotel bar was well known as a gay hookup venue, too, so it didn't take much imagination for the gentleman across the room to assume that Gene was a rent-boy.

Dinner was nearing its completion and Gene knew that Oscar and Ricardo would make excuses at any moment about leaving while suggesting that Salisbury and Gene remain for another drink—afterwards, of course . . .

Feeling a bit panicked, needing to bolster his courage, and having an urge to piss, Gene excused himself for the opportunity to go to the men's room before the real event started. The eyes of the gentleman across the room followed him to the door.

And when Gene was in the men's room and standing at a urinal and pissing into it, he found that the gentleman followed him there too. They stood side-by-side for longer than necessary, both with their dicks out, each man's cock in view of the other man. Gene was pleased to see that the man was hung. The man smiled—not into Gene's face—but looking down at his cock, so it was evident that he liked what he saw too. Both had completed their urination, but they both just stood there, waiting for something.

The man moved first. He pulled away from his urinal. Gene felt the disappointment of the loss of him, but only for a second or two because the man didn't leave. In a whisper behind Gene, the man said, "Is your time for sale, and are you available?"

Gene murmured a "Maybe, for the right man."

"Could I be the right man?"

"Yes."

The man came in close behind Gene and embraced him, one hand going to Gene's belly and the other fisting his cock.

"Do you mind?" he whispered in Gene's ear. "I want to make you come, and I want to fuck you. Do you mind?"

"Not at all," Gene murmured and he leaned a bit forward, placing the palms of his hands against the tiles of the wall behind the urinals. He nearly laughed at the similarity between this afternoon in the abandoned park restroom and here. The circumstances were so different and yet his arousal was the same.

The man was stroking Gene's cock off. His face was buried in Gene's neck. He kissed the young man, blew in his ear, and whispered, "If I'm going to be fucking you, we should know each other's names. I am Kenton. Kenton Blackburn. And you are Beautiful and Submissive Young Man. That's the name I will know you by. You *are* submissive, aren't you?"

Gene laughed, a low guttural laugh. "Yes, I'm submissive. I'm Gene. Gene Worth. From New York."

"You're one of the models who came in for the fashion show up in the Stag Club earlier today, aren't you?"

"Yes, and you're going to make me come quickly if you don't stop jacking me off," Gene said.

"That's the plan. Fire when ready. And I want to fuck you then. I could fuck you right here, but we could be discovered at any moment. The danger of that is arousing in itself, though, isn't it?"

"Yes, yes, it is, and it's going to make me come. Oh, shit. Fuck. I am coming."

And then he did, splashing his spunk against the back wall of the urinal. He turned his face to the man's—to Kenton Blackburn's face—and they kissed.

"Is your name really Kenton Blackburn?" Gene whispered.

"Yes. Half the arousal is knowing that it really will be Kenton Blackburn fucking you. Are you really Gene Worth of New York City?"

"Yes."

"Thanks for being honest. I saw a program from the fashion show today. I knew you really were Gene Worth. I like that you were honest with me. I do want to fuck you— and to save you from that ogre at your table. You don't really want to be there, do you? You are going with that loser because Oscar Oliphant wants you to—that Oliphant will profit from you doing so, aren't you?"

"Yes."

"But you will go with me instead and lay under me, won't you?"

"Yes."

"Don't be fooled by appearances. I will be rough."

"That will be fine. I'll have to admit that I've become jaded to vanilla sex."

"I will test you. I know a back way to get to the hotel lobby without going back to the bar. I could get a room here."

"I already have a room here," Gene whispered.

* * * *

Blackburn was riding him high on the bed in a doggie. Gene's chest was pushed into the mattress and his arms were flung out to the side, his fists gripping bunches of the bedspread. He was raised on his knees, his tail high in the air, and the older man was riding him hard, leaning over him, smashing Gene's cheek into the bedspread with one hand and whipping his exposed buttocks and thighs with his belt with the other as he thrust hard inside him, again and again.

Gene was loving the intensity of the ride.

Despite the check on whether Gene would take the fuck rough, that it was an extra-rough fuck had arisen from a misunderstanding, but Gene hadn't corrected the impression Blackburn had gotten. After standing and kissing and fondling each other, pulling their cocks out while still dressed and stroking each other to high arousal, they had undressed each other and laid on the bed. There was only one table lamp on, and that was across the room, so it was dim where the bed was.

Blackburn had started off making tender love to Gene, kissing him all over and running his hands on the young man's curves and into his crevices. While he did so, though, he discovered the light welts on Gene's buttocks and back and the burn marks on his wrists.

"You've had it rough recently," he remarked. He was kissing and licking the welts down from Gene's back and onto his buttocks.

"Yes," Gene whispered.

"And you liked it rough," Blackburn said.

"Yes," Gene admitted.

"But you'll take it even rougher than that?"

"Yes." He gave a little cry because Blackburn then flipped him over on his back, laced his arms through Gene's thighs, and raised and spread them. The cry was because the man had gone immediately for his hole with his tongue and teeth. He backed off occasionally, biting Gene on his tender-skin inner thighs. And then he was kneeling between Gene's thighs, shoving his knees under Gene's buttocks. There had been little preparation and his dick was big. Still, while he was binding Gene's wrists together over his head with Gene's belt, he was working his cock inside the young man's channel.

Gene writhed under him, panting hard, and crying out "Fuck, shit, fuck!" but Blackburn gave him no quarter, as he assumed Gene wanted. In short order, with Blackburn deep inside Gene, they established a coordinated rhythm of the fuck and Gene was crying out for the thrusting. Somehow Blackburn had managed to sheath himself before penetrating Gene's ass and when he came, he pulled away from Gene, ripped the spent condom off, arced three prodigious gobs of cum on Gene's heaving belly, and managed to dunk toss the condom in the waste basket beside the bed.

They lay there, tangled up with each other, both panting hard.

"Hot damn," Blackburn murmured.

"Fuckin' A right," Gene whispered. Blackburn released Gene's wrists from the binding of the belt and flicked it against Gene's flanks. The younger man scooted down the bed and took Blackburn's cock in his mouth and sucked it hard again. When the older man was fully erect again, Gene sat up and looked down into his face and smiled. Blackburn smiled back and then backhanded Gene across the cheek, sending the young man sprawling back on the bed in surprise.

That's when Blackburn positioned Gene for the doggie and mounted and fucked his ass, while he strapped him lightly with the belt.

Afterward they lay stretched out beside each other on the bed, each working at bringing their heavy breathing under control.

"Did I do it right?" Blackburn whispered.

"You did it great. But you should know that I don't usually have it that rough. Earlier was just something unusual."

"I'm sorry then. I don't usually give it that rough. Maybe I didn't—"

"It was great. I'd like to have it that way from time to time. It makes me feel alive. As I said, I take men's cocks so often, that it can become boring vanilla sex. I felt alive with you."

"Will I see you again—fuck you again?"

"If you live in New York or come to New York."

"I live here in Chicago. But I go to New York sometimes."

"I have address cards over on the desk," Gene said. "I'm going to go take a shower now, but you can take one of my cards and call me when you come to New York. I'd like that."

"Let me shower first," Blackburn said, rolling off the bed. It was a command, not a request. He was asserting full control.

The knock at the door—more like a bang—startled them both. The voice of Ricardo boomed out. "Are you in there, Gene? Open up. Where the fuck did you go?"

The bang rang out again but then was followed by a more gentle knock. Oscar Oliphant this time. "You there, baby? Don't be scared. It's OK. I know he is a toad. It's OK. We closed the deal anyway. I see that you've been hurt, though. Open up, baby. Tell me what happened."

With a sigh, Gene rolled over and sat on the side of the bed, but Blackburn gestured for him to stay there. He was already standing half way to the door. He leaned down, scarfed up his briefs, pulled them on, and went to the door. He opened it. Oscar and Ricardo were on the other side, out in the corridor. Their faces showed surprise and then narrowed into a frown. They backed up as Blackburn moved into the corridor and pulled the door nearly shut behind him.

Gene heard voices from the other side of the door, Ricardo talking in anger at first but the tone calming down. Gene couldn't hear what they were saying. He opened the drawer to the nightstand and pulled out a pack of cigarettes, extracted one, and lit it up. His hand was shaking, but he didn't know whether that had been from the rough sex or the appearance of Oscar. He was aware he'd let Oscar down. He was more aware that he didn't give a shit that he had. He sensed that his Oscar and Ricardo period might be coming to an end.

Blackburn reentered the room, raised a finger to stave off questions, rummaged around in the separate parts of his tux on the carpet and came up with a check book and a pen from the inside pocket of his tux jacket. He went back into the corridor. When he returned, he walked over to stand in front of where Gene was sitting. He tossed the check book and pen on the nightstand, gently took the cigarette out of Gene's mouth, took a puff himself, and ground the cigarette into the ashtray on the nightstand. He cupped Gene's face with his hand and came in for a kiss.

Coming out of the kiss, he looked into Gene's eyes, and said, "It seems you are mine now. Bought and paid for. You weren't cheap and I always get my money's worth."

Gene was totally surprised by the slap. Blackburn backhanded him across his cheek, sending him flopping back onto the bed. Blackburn stripped off his briefs, grabbed Gene's ankles in his fists, wishboned the young man's legs, and dove between them. He thrust inside Gene hard and deep, and the young man arched his back and his head and grabbed for Blackburn's hair, hanging on for dear life and writhing, panting hard, and groaning his total surrender, as the older man pistoned him to a bareback creaming. The frame of the bed shimmered and complained as their pelvises bounced up and down, Blackburn driving hard, and Gene meeting him in counterthrusts. They came almost simultaneously, both in a joyous shout.

Pulling out of him, Blackburn said, "OK, you can shower first." He took a cigarette from the pack Gene had left on the nightstand, lit up, and went to the window, turned away from Gene, while Gene groaned in the effort to rise from the bed and stumble to the bathroom. Despite the groan, he couldn't help having a little smile on his face. God, the man could fuck.

When Gene came out of the bathroom, he found Blackburn, dressed again, sitting at the desk, reading his manuscript.

"Is this yours? Did you write this?"

"Yes," Gene said. "I'm studying to be a writer."

"Well this is good—no, it's very good. I'm a book publisher. Here in Chicago. That's what I do. I know good when I see it. I would publish this. No, if you let me, I *will* publish this."

"You really think its publishable?"

"Yes. You have to stay in Chicago for a while. You have to come home with me. Tonight. We have to start work on this. Sign contracts. Get started."

"You're not just trying to get me into your bed, are you?" Gene asked.

"Well, yes, but I want your book too."

"You want to fuck my book?"

"No, I want to publish your book. And I want to fuck you too. Pack your bag. My car is in the hotel garage."

Blackburn's car was a sleek BMW 7 series. His mansion was nearly an hour west in a wealthy suburb. He wasn't married. They fucked in the first bedroom they came to. The bed was huge. And despite his age Blackburn was able to get it up, stick it in, and fire it off two more times before the grandfather clock in his foyer downstairs struck midnight.

Gene rolled off the bed and walked for what seemed to be a mile before he got to the voluminous master bedroom. Once there, he took a shower and then stood at the urinal—the bathroom was fancy enough to have a urinal as well as a toilet and even a bidet—and took a piss. Blackburn, naked, came into the bath. He moved in close behind Gene, palmed Gene's belly with one hand, and encircled the young man's cock with the other. Gene leaned in, stiff arming and palming the wall behind the urinal, letting Blackburn hold his cock for the finish of the urination. The older man didn't take his hand away then, though. He began stroking Gene's cock.

"I wanted to fuck you at the urinal at the hotel bar," he whispered.

"Yes," Gene whispered.

"I want to fuck you here, now, at the urinal," Blackburn said.

"Yes," Gene answered.

Blackburn kissed him on the neck, took his hand away from Gene's belly long enough to wedge his sheathed cockhead in Gene's channel entrance, and then moved his hand back. He pressed in on Gene's belly while he thrust up into Gene's channel with his hard cock. Gene grimaced, but he took the penetration without jerking. He knew it was Sunday for no other reason than he'd had a cock up his ass for most of the day. He wasn't complaining, though.

As he slow pumped Gene's ass and stroked off his cock, the older man whispered in Gene's ear, "Thank you. I so wanted to do this back in the bar."

"I was dying for you to do it there too," Gene murmured.

"You are completely submissive to me."

"Yes," Gene answered.

"I like that. I'll make it worth your while."

When they had both come, Blackburn went into the shower and Gene returned to the bed.

That was Sunday in Chicago, he mused to himself as he drifted off, contented, satiated, and encouraged that his writer career was already taking off, close in the embrace of the book publisher, Kenton Blackburn.

Gene didn't give much thought at all to having deserted Oscar Oliphant back at the bar. Instead he felt the exhilaration of having greater control of his own life. He had burned his bridges before.

Chapter Four: Los Angeles Sunday

"Isn't this romantic?"

Gene looked over at Aaron Trimble to see if he was being sarcastic, but he looked like the comment was straight. They were late getting to the ranch party up beyond Santa Clarita on I-5 toward the Los Padres National Forest, because Gene's agent was anxious to pull off into a rest stop so that Gene could give him a behind-the-wheel blow job. To Gene it was considered paying the rent and Trimble, though twenty years older than Gene, had a nice enough cock, and this was after all Sunday. Gene had long thought of Sunday as an "easy day"—one on which he would let himself be easily made.

Trimble's excuse had been, "You look good enough to eat. Like bees to the honey, baby. With you it's like bees to the honey—especially dressed like that."

It hadn't been Trimble who'd done any eating though. He'd force fed Gene his cock.

Trimble had been the one to tell Gene what to wear to the party—where Gene was supposed to hook up with an assistant producer who was sitting on his novel manuscript, holding it hostage for getting filming started because he wanted something from Gene first. The clothes were from Gene's House of Oliphant period. While Gene was modeling there, he got to keep most of the clothes he wore on the catwalk. This was from Oliphant's adult male collection—the one he'd shown in Chicago five months earlier, the last time Gene had seen Oliphant. Oliphant had sent Gene's stuff out to Chicago, to Kenton Blackburn, Gene's publisher and new master—at least that's how Gene saw it—after Gene left his fashion house.

The top was a cut-off black mesh athletic T, rendered in shiny material and showing Gene's very nice six pack. Below he was wearing skimpy, red silk athletic shorts over a red silk jock strap. His feet were in sandals. He'd come out of Trimble's Santa Monica beach house with a small red swimsuit, but Trimble had said he wouldn't need it despite the fact that they were going to a pool party. Gene tossed it in the backseat of the car anyway, just in case.

Trimble was pointing to a hilltop they were passing on I-5. "Looks like Tuscany, doesn't it? It's a winery. Have you ever been to Italy, Gene?"

"I've been to the Little Italy section of New York City," Gene answered.

Trimble laughed. "You need to get around more."

"If you'd get this movie deal on solid ground, I'd be happy to do the world tour. I could write my next novel."

"Patience, little guy, patience."

Gene was out of patience after five months out here with the sale of his novel to the movies being on again and off again, often determined by how recently he'd been laid on some movie mogul's audition coach. Who knew how many of these fuckers out here fucked young male hopefuls? Even Aaron Trimble, the general agent Kenton Blackburn had brought Gene out to L.A. to hook up with to handle the movie rights sales had had him on his office coach and by his pool and in his bed—and now, when he felt like it—in the pool house at the Santa Monica beach house. Trimble was giving Gene a room in exchange for privileges. Gene was making ends meet while he waited for something to happen on the movie deal by renting his body out.

If Gene hadn't made the room-in-exchange-for-sex deal with Trimble, he'd have run out of money long before this. He'd spent his advance money on the novel quickly out here, which wasn't hard to do. There would be more when the royalties came in—the novel was selling well enough for this dickering to happen on movie rights—but that wouldn't start for a few more months.

Gene had essentially been abandoned in Los Angeles. Blackburn had brought him out here, saying they'd have a deal quickly. But he hadn't told Gene what "quickly" meant in California parlance. Gene and Blackburn had reached a parting of sexual interest fairly quickly, though. Blackburn had discovered he had more of an appetite for rough sex than he had realized and Gene had discovered that he didn't. So Blackburn was back in Chicago now. Gene was still in his stable of writers, and was working on a second novel, but they were waving at each other from half a continent's separation.

Now it was Hollywood and Gene trying to scrape up enough money to get back to New York. Today was attending to two needs at once. One of the last hurdles in formally signing a movie deal on the novel was a producer, Cory Kadowski, who had signaled his interest in Gene. And Trimble had worked out that they could get to Kadowski today, as he would be at a ranch pool party up near Santa Clarita by also taking care of the expressed interest in Gene by the ranch's owner and party host.

"You only have to do two of them today," Trimble said, as he roared past the Tuscan-style winery compound on the hill overlooking I-5. "It's a stag party, though, just men into men and boys. I've gotten you in as one of the roaming chickens—guys like you who look young but aren't too young and will lay around with their legs open to any guest wanting to plug them. But if you let anyone other than Kadowski and Danner do you, that's up to you. I'll be playing elsewhere. I can have you at home."

"You make it sound so delicious," Gene said.

"This is where the world of fake meets the world of reality, kid," Trimble said, with a laugh. "You're just fortunate that you got looks and the right pheromones—

honey to the bee, that's you. You got a leg up on most other young guys out here. With you, it's just like honey for the bees."

"I've heard something like that before."

"You're just lucky you got both Kadowski and Danner who want to get into your pants. We're just about home free on this. Kadowski's that last cock that needs sucked, I promise."

"I sure hope so," Gene said. "I'm just about tapped out."

"Not like most young guys out here," Trimble shot back. "As long as you take my cock, you've got a roof over your head in L.A. That's more than most young hopefuls can say out here."

"Yeah, yeah, yeah."

The door of the ranch house was opened to them by a butler, but the rancher himself, Cliff Danner, a regular star of an L.A.-based soap opera was close behind, glad handing them into the house, welcoming them both but with his eyes plastered to Gene only, obviously liking what he saw.

Danner had been on the soap opera for over twenty years, his character having developed from a young, teenage heartthrob who was making a mother out of all of the young girls drifting in and out of the script plots to one of three brothers vying for control of a Mafia-financed international restaurant chain upon the death of the family patriarch. This storyline had been approached and retreated from on the television program for the last two years.

Danner was in his late forties, and he had aged extremely well, thanks to all of the handling and sculpting and grooming that the television studio could apply. He was thickening a bit around the middle but, thanks to careful attention to his six pack, he was on his way to becoming a Zeus rather than a fatty, and he had retained his chiseled ruggedly good looks and a healthy head of now gray-blond hair. He was just wearing a Speedo, flip-flops, and a beer can. This was a pool party. The distinctive curve left down his thigh in the Speedo material made quite clear that he was hung, which had helped him maintain position in his role over the years. He had a hairy chest, but it was tastefully groomed. He looked handsome, tanned, and plastic. It fit right in to Hollywood.

A large number of very expensive cars had been parked haphazardly around a large graveled motor court at the front of the house, and Gene and Trimble had been able to hear a raucous party going on in the pool area at the back of the house. They could tell what sort of party this was before they even got to the door. Two men, the bottom young and the top middle-aged, were fucking on the hood of a Lexus convertible not far from the front entry.

"Hal Taggert is here, out at the pool, Aaron, and said he wanted to know the minute you arrived. He wants to talk to you." Danner was speaking to Trimble, but he was looking at Gene and had a hand on the young man's forearm. "I'm sure that your young friend here would like a tour of the house before I bring him out."

"Did Cory Kadowski come? Has he arrived yet?" Trimble asked somewhat anxiously.

"Yes, he's here, but I want it first," Danner answered.

There wasn't much question in Gene's view what getting a tour of the ranch house would entail.

He was quite right. The house of huge, of course. It had a bedroom level that a small hotel would be proud of. Danner showed Gene a couple of the rooms with beds, including the master bedroom. At another one in a wing away from the pool terrace, He stopped, and said, "This is a room that you alone can use today. You'll find there are restraints on the bed, if . . . I've heard Cory . . . well . . . you know. God, you're beautiful," he suddenly added. He pulled Gene to him, slipping the black mesh belly T over his head as he did so, and they went into a kissing and fondling embrace there in the doorway to the bedroom.

"Here? Now?" Gene asked.

"Yes, quickly," Danner answered, his voice breathy.

It wasn't long until Danner's Speedo slipped to the floor and Gene went down on his knees in front of him and took the TV star's cock in his mouth.

The bedroom had its own en suite commodious marble-lined bathroom. Danner fucked Gene on the bathroom vanity. Gene was perched on the expanse of marble between two wash basins, his tail on the front edge of the ledge, his shoulder blades pressed into the mirrored wall behind the vanity, and his ankles on Danner's shoulders as, leaving Gene in his red silk jock strap, which didn't encumber access to Gene's channel by Danner's thick cock in the least, the TV star pounded away at Gene's ass . . . and pounded and pounded and pounded. He kept looking over Gene's shoulder into the mirror, admiring his role as a top. Once a TV actor always a TV actor.

The man had marvelous control and took his time, giving all of his attention to Gene even though there were maybe a hundred guests and rent-boys downstairs at the pool party he was hosting.

Gene went with him, showing him a good time, taking the cock deep, moving his pelvis with the rhythm of the fuck, telling the man he was a master and was killing him—but killing him good.

"You're very good. I want to see you again," Danner said when they were back in the bedroom and pulling their scant clothes back on. "If Kadowski signs off on your movie deal, you owe me, and I'll collect," he added.

"Yes, sir, I understand," Gene answered.

At the door, Danner turned and said. "If I want you to stay the night, after the party, you will, won't you?"

"If you want," Gene responded. "I'd like that," he added, knowing it's what Danner wanted to hear and what his agent, Trimble, would want Gene to say—unless Kadowski wanted to take Gene home with him.

One down, at least for now, Gene thought. And it wasn't so bad. One more to go. But, what the hell, it's easy Sunday.

* * * *

Gene's head was spinning and the world below him was swirling with the bodies of men in all of the colors of the rainbow dancing around the swimming pool. He had taken the pills offered to him when he was by the pool and the gross whale had his flippers around him and was pulling him to the house, but he didn't do drugs—usually. He wouldn't have taken them normally. But it seems he did. The world around him was in a slow churn and his head felt like it was lifting off his body. But he didn't care. He was happy. Why would he take? . . . Oh, right, a slimy rhino was pulling him to the house. Anything to counter the expectation of where that was leading.

The window pane behind the headboard of the bed he was riding the rhino on was cool, and he alternated between pressing his cheek and his forehead to it. When he pressed his forehead to it, he could look down into the pool area, where the party was in full swing with the undulating figures of all of the beautiful men revolving to the throbbing beat in his brain. But not all of the men were beautiful. Some were fat and old and gross—and grabby. And it wasn't a rhino he was riding. It was the gross man's face. He was sitting on Cory Kadowski's face, and the rhino was gripping his waist and eating his ass out.

Then Gene was scrabbling at the window behind the headboard as he was being pulled away. And then he was being pulled from the brass top rung of the headboard. He was sliding down the gross man's hairy chest, dragged up and over his huge belly. Gene was the size of a mere child

91

in contrast to this blubbery mountain of a man. The man had the strength to do whatever he wanted with him, though. And the man was doing that—positioning his anus over the man's erect club. Gene was howling as his ass was lowered onto Kadowski's cock. He had the cock of a bull, a horse, an elephant. Gene's head was throbbing and spinning with all the swirl of colors. His ass hurt like hell. It was spread to the limit of splitting by a throbbing baseball bat. But Gene was laughing, calling out, "Fuck me, big boy! Give it to me with that monster cock, daddy!" as he was being lifted and slammed down, lifted and slammed down.

He swiveled on the cock, grabbing for the headboard, his knees dug into the mattress on either side of the tub of lard, using his knees as levers to rise and fall, rise and fall, fucking himself on the monster shaft, his body reversed on the reclining whale. He was looking at anything he could other than the massive, jiggling mound of flesh under him. He concentrated on the cock—on being able to ride it. That, at least, was arousing—to be able to sheath it and service it.

Kadowski lay on his back, head toward the headboard, feet toward the footboard, with Gene now on top of him, pointed at and grasping the top of the brass rung footboard with his hands. The fat man still gripped Gene by the waist and, in consort with Gene's leveraging off his knees to rise and fall, pulled him back and forth hard on his cock, grunting and groaning, while Gene moaned and cried out and watched all the pretty colors swirling before his throbbing head—and delivered as promised.

* * * *

Earlier than that, after the TV actor, Cliff Danner, fucked Gene in the guestroom bathroom and had left him, Gene took a shower, pulled his clothes back on, and went down to where the party by the pool was in full swing.

He moved around the terrace, smiling at other guests, flirting with them, and politely, with smiles, slipping away from groping hands as he walked the perimeter of the pool, getting his bearings. It was Sunday; he could let loose on Sundays and pretend the rest of the week that he hadn't. Most of the men were beautiful and muscular and California tanned. He would have happily gone with most of the men here with they were the movie producer he'd been brought here to fuck. None of the good-looking men at the pool were Kadowski, though, and Gene knew they weren't.

Most of them were uninhibited this late in the party as well. As many were naked as were wearing bathing suits, and the naked ones almost universally were hung, whether they were young, old, or middle aged. Some of them were "chickens," as Gene was deemed to be. These were young looking and were there to service the men buzzing around them and manhandling them. The least inhibited ones were fucking. The hedonist atmosphere and scent of spunk and testosterone floating across the pool area was contagious.

Gene's beautiful small body was getting attention with the bold colors of the shiny black mesh belly T and red silk mini shorts he wore as he walked the rim of the pool, and frenzy only increased when he slipped off the shorts and was just wearing the red silk jock strap below.

He accepted drinks—more than he should have—but staved off the free-flowing offer of brightly colored pills—at least to that point.

The bona fide party took note of Gene when he drew near and buzzed around him Gene like bees to the honey just as his agent had said they would. Gene recognized a few of them from TV. Two of them, in particular, a Jeff and a Steve, were ones that Gene melted to when he saw them on TV. He stop beside them and gave them a smile. In just pausing and acknowledging Steve's catcall, Gene was saying "yes." Jeff embraced him from the front and Steve from the back. Steve murmured in Gene's ear, "Can you hear the music? Dance with us."

"It could be fun to do you together," Jeff said as the three of them were dancing together beside the pool to the beat of rock music, naked and hung Jeff in front of Gene and hung and naked Steve close behind Gene. The three were laughing and flirting and trying to keep the drinks in their glasses from sloshing out as them writhed against each other's bodies.

"You can if you like," Gene answered. His agent said he could take whatever pleasure he wanted from the party as long as he fucked the two men he was here to service.

"Seriously?" Steve said. "You're just shitting us, aren't you? You do doubles?"

"Sure, I do." Gene answered. That was the truth. He did.

"Prove it," Jeff challenged.

Gene, having had two drinks too many, did prove it. It was a chore, because they were both bigger than the average, but Gene was open from Danner's cocking and the relaxing effect of the drinks, and he managed them. And he enjoyed managing them. Steve sank to the adjacent chaise lounge, bringing Gene down with him, as, standing behind Gene, Jeff ran his hands under the waistband of Gene's jock strap and pulled it down his legs.

Jeff and Steve fucked him together on a chaise lounge bed, Steve on his back on the bottom, holding Gene's small, lithe body on top of him and fucking up into Gene's passage, and Jeff straddling the lounge bed behind Gene, palming the young man's belly, and pumping Gene's ass above the buried cock of Steve. The black mesh T went the way of the red silk jock strap. Gene was naked in all his glory, a glory that voyeurs applauded as they gathered around to watch him be double fucked by the two naked hunks. Gene had a nice cock, which onlookers took turns stroking while he was being fucked, but it didn't rival any of those swinging free around him. It certainly didn't match up with either Steve's or Jeff's.

Toward the grand finale three-way shoot off, Gene froze for an instant, recognizing someone on the other side of the pool. But this had progressed too far for him not to get back into the action of two big cocks on two gorgeous young television personalities churning inside him, and Gene shelved the surprise viewing and went with the glorious fuck.

"Hello, Manny," Gene said when he'd worked his way to the other side of the pool later. "I certainly didn't expect to see you here, although I guess I shouldn't have been surprised." The man Gene had seen from across the pool that had given him pause in the middle of the double penetration fuck by the two TV hunks was his roommate in New York of three years earlier, Manuel Rodrigues, a fashion house photographer by day and a porn filmmaker by night. Gene had needed money enough that he'd been in a couple of Manny's films. He'd also been in Manny's bed.

"I think I was the more surprised of the two," Manny said. "I never figured you as ever being outside of New York. You're lookin' good and I see that you're as easy as ever. I saw you earlier, but seein' as how you were the meat of a big boy sandwich, I didn't interrupt."

"You're looking good too," Gene said. He was being polite and they both knew it. Manny hadn't aged well over the last three years, and he'd gone to fat.

"Good enough that you'll go over in those bushes and let me hump you—for old time's sake?" They both laughed, but there was no reason for Gene not to think Manny was serious. He'd always been randy, ready to go at any time. He was wearing swimming trunks now, but his erection was pushing them out. He might had gained weight, but his cock most likely was still highly rideable. He'd given Gene some good times.

"I'm on assignment. You wouldn't know the movie producer Cory Kadowski and be able to point him out, would you?"

"Shit. Kadowski's an ogre. What do you have to do for him and why?"

"I have to lay down for him. You know that novel I was working on? It's been published and the movie rights deal is making the rounds here. Kadowski is a stumbling block. My agent says I have to fuck him to get the manuscript moving up the ladder again."

"He's a monster, I hear--Kadowski. A real Frankenstein and a bull to boot. And sadistic, I hear. You probably want to stay clear of him."

"I can't, I'm afraid. I need the money from a movie deal. Is he here?"

"Yes. He's over there talking to that shitty agent, Aaron Trimble. The fat guy in the baggy blue trunks."

"Fuck," Gene said when he looked over there. "You're right. He's a whale. And you're right about Trimble being a shitty agent too. He's the agent handling my movie deal."

"Listen," Manny said, "if it's money you need and you don't want to do it with Kadowski or be controlled by Trimble, maybe I can help you."

"You? How?"

"You asked what I'm doing out here. The porn films took off and I have a very lucrative Internet site now. You were good in the films—very popular. You need money, you can make a lot of money in porn fast. So, if you're nice to me, I'd be happy to take you on and set you up in a film fast. I'd pay you for it just as fast."

"We'll see how this other deal goes," Gene said. But he wasn't a dummy. He hadn't done too well so far by burning bridges or not keeping options open. "How nice?" he asked.

"Those bushes are still over there, and you make me horny as hell," Manny said, with a smile

Manny doggie fucked him in the bushes—and they weren't alone or the only ones fucking in the bushes by the pool. Gene didn't have to think of him as having gone to fat. He was as strong as ever and he had the same expert cock. He came in behind Gene, had the young man bend over and grab his ankles, and Manny grabbed Gene's hips between his hands, mounted and penetrated him, and took him swiftly and deep. Gene was yawning open from having just done a double, so he had no trouble with Manny's shaft and enjoyed the filmmaker's cocking technique.

When they emerged from the bushes, Kadowski and Trimble were still in conversation across the pool. Trimble saw Gene and waved him over. Before he left, Manny said, "Good luck. Offer's open. You're honey to the bees. You still have the same e-mail address as in New York?"

"Yes," Gene answered.

"So, I'll contact you to establish a connection."

"We'll see," said Gene as he gave a deep sigh, fought for a smile he could give for the fat ogre watching him from across the pool, and did the long walk.

"This is Mr. Kadowski," Trimble said as Gene reached them. Gene gave the mountain of a man a wan smile and resisted jumping away from him when he put a flipper—a hand—on Gene's forearm.

Just then a serving guy passed by them carrying a silver tray with an array of bright-colored pills on it.

"Mood aids, anyone?" the server asked, and fluttered his eyelashes at Aaron Trimble. He instantly identified Gene as another bottom, and he avoided looking at Kadowski. Trimble looked like a good top to him.

"I'll take a blue one and a green one," Gene squeaked, already regretting having agreed to let the movie producer lay him.

"Then you can show me what's inside the house," Kadowski said. "Cliff Danner told me we had the use of a room in there."

"Sure," Gene said, popping the pills in his mouth and downing them with the beer he took from Trimble's hand.

* * * *

After the first fuck, Kadowski moved on to more personal pleasures with Gene. He found the restraints tucked under the mattress of the bed in the guest bedroom they'd been lent. In fact, while Gene was engaged in a panting recovery from the reverse cowboy ride Kadowski had taken him on, the movie producer had gone looking for the restraints. So, Danner must have told him they were there for his use.

He spread-eagled Gene on his belly on the bed, stretching his arms and legs up and out, restrained to the corners of the bed. Then he stuffed pillows under Gene's belly, raising the young man's buttocks to complete vulnerability and access to him. He crouched over Gene's buttocks, grabbing the young man's waist between his hands, and laughed at the cry and jerk Gene gave when he thrust inside Gene's ass. And then he rode him and fucked him, rode him and fucked him, rode him and fucked him. Half way through the ride, he leaned over far enough to take Gene's throat in a two-handed choke hold and finished the fuck combining breath play with pelvis thrusts.

The movie producer might have been a gross, fat pig, but he was strong, virile, and long-lasting. He knew what he wanted and he took it.

Gene was left trussed up, panting and moaning, while Kadowski went for a shower. When he returned, he unbound the young man. But he didn't do so until he had pulled his bathing suit back on and was ready to leave.

98

He didn't say "thank you" or "good job" or anything like that. Right before leaving—leaving the party altogether and roaring away in the back of his black Bentley salon car—he did say, "I've read most of your novel. It's suitable for filming. Have your agent drop by my office on Tuesday morning."

That was the last Gene ever heard from Cory Kadowski.

Gene lay there, recovering, beyond the filtering away of the party guests from the pool below. At length, all was quiet and the sounds of the cars departing from the front motor court died down. Cliff Danner entered the room.

"Aaron Trimble has gone back to L.A.," he said. "He'll return for you tomorrow." He then came over to the bed and, to the sound of Gene's groans, picked the young man up, slung him over his shoulder, padded to the master bedroom, dumped Gene on the master bed, and fucked him some more in a missionary and then a doggie and then . . .

* * * *

The naked hunk was sitting in the driver's seat of the classic white 1974 Corvette Stingray convertible, his legs out of the car. The driver's door was open and his right leg was hung over the top of that, the window down. His left leg, the heel of his foot pressed into the grass was stretched out straight. His right arm was bent over the top of the windshield. The fingers of his left hand were buried in Gene Worth's wind-ruffled hair.

The Stingray was parked on the top of a cliff overlooking the Pacific Ocean. Jagged rocks heaved up out of the restless surf in the cove below, highlighting the rugged terrain of the California coast. No civilization was in sight.

Gene, naked, knelt on the grass between the hunk's spread legs, giving the hunk a blow job.

The scene faded out and then back in to Gene spread-eagled over the trunk of the Corvette, his legs crouched in the limited space behind the driver's and passenger's seats, his chest pressed into the trunk of the car, and his arms stretched out, his hands reaching for the car's taillights on either side. The hunk was standing in the well of the car behind the seats and hovering over Gene's back. His right hand was buried in Gene's hair, pulling Gene's head back brutally and arching the young man's back. His left hand was grasping Gene's waist. He was fucking Gene's ass in long strokes with a long, thick cock. The cock thrusts, with the view over the sea behind the tableau of the two beautiful men fucking, were clearly visible from the perspective of the land side of the car.

Manny Rodriguez had two other cameramen with him on the photo shoot, and they videoed the action from every angle they could without getting themselves or their shadows into any of the frames. Manny had told the hunk, a guy with classic California beach bum looks picked up on Malibu Beach who did occasional films for him, and Gene generally what he wanted in the movie. It wasn't anything new really. It started with Gene hitchhiking and being picked up by the hunk in his Corvette. There were meaningful looks between the two in the car and then they went immediately to the blow job scene on the cliff top and the fuck. The last scene was the only thing new. That was a shot of Gene driving the Corvette down the coastal road and the hunk nowhere in sight.

Maybe some of the viewers would be left wondering what the story on that was. Whether after being mastered and ravished, the Gene character somehow came out on top with the nice sports car. But the main thing was that both men were gorgeous and they looked good fucking. That's what the viewers would be paying for.

This was the second movie Gene had done for Manny, each on successive Sundays. When Aaron Trimble had gone to Cory Kadowski's office the Tuesday after Cliff Danner's pool party, he was told that Kadowski had flown out to London on Monday and would get in touch with Trimble for the next time Gene could "consult" with him on the movie deal.

Gene gave up at that point. After this movie he'd have the travel money he needed.

For now, though, they were wrapping up this movie. Gene already knew that after the film was in the can Manny would take him to some sleazy hotel nearby and bang the hell of him and not return him to Aaron Trimble until Monday morning.

"Can't help it, baby," Manny would say. "You're like honey to the bees. And you're so easy."

"Only on Sunday, Manny," Gene would say. They'd been here before.

But it *was* Sunday. Sunday in Los Angeles.

* * * *

It wasn't a Sunday. It was a Tuesday. Gene Worth had been back in New York City for nearly a week. Manny hadn't given up his apartment—the one Gene had lived in with him—because it was rent controlled and Manny didn't know whether or how long he'd be staying out in California. He'd given the key to Gene. Gene had spent the week becoming reacclimated to the city and wondering why he'd ever left New York to begin with.

He hadn't gone out for easy sex on Sunday. He'd stayed in and written on his new novel. He'd made great progress on that, he thought. He already was getting pushy e-mails from his publisher, Kenton Blackburn, in Chicago about receiving a prospectus on what Gene was writing. None of the e-mails had hinted of sex, though, and Gene surmised that whatever sexual relationship he'd had with Blackburn now was over. That was a bit sad, but the professional relationship still was there. Perhaps, Gene thought, he was maturing to not having to have a submissive relationship involved in every professional relationship he had with a man.

For some reason that made him think of Josh Steinem, the fashion designer and literary journal publisher who lived in the five-story brownstone on 39th Street. He kept thinking that that was one man he could have a balanced sexual and professional relationship with. That man had treated him right. And perhaps he'd thought about Josh because of Saturday, when he had gone to Central Park aching for sex—he was highly sexed; there was nothing he could do about that or wanted to change about that—and had taken a man back to the apartment and had been treated as well as Josh had treated him.

His name was Tray. He was black, and tall and slim and well-muscled and wore his hair in long, black dreadlocks. He was a sidewalk poet and, for all Gene knew, homeless. Gene had heard him reciting poetry at the side of a path in the park, standing there with a hat turned in front of him and giving a bright white-toothed smile to everyone who dropped coins in his hat in passing. Gene had heard him from afar and been drawn to the rich baritone and mesmerizing cadence of his words as he recited his strong beat and clever rhyming poetry of an heroic rescue at sea by brave and gloriously described coastal patrol members of the Jersey shore in the previous century.

This theme closely paralleled the setting and background of the new novel Gene was working on, so he sat in a bench on the other side of the poet and listened to him, letting the words roll over him, and, unconsciously perhaps, taking bits and pieces of what he was hearing and letting them insert themselves in what he was forming in his mind to write. It is very likely that the poet Tray provided the inspiration that made Gene's writing the next day so fluid and so enriching to the building theme of the novel.

The two men eyed each other, and at some point Tray was speaking directly to Gene and reaching into the young man's soul. The attraction was unmistakable and unavoidable. Tray was quite obviously a sensual man and Gene had come to the park seeking sexual release. Tray looked directly into Gene's eyes and one of his hands dropped to his crotch and he fondled himself invitingly. Gene rose from his bench, walked across the path, dropped a fifty-dollar bill in Tray's hat, and stood up and waited.

"You want me to go with you somewhere?" the black man asked.

"Yes," Gene answered.

"I give cock. Do you take cock?"

"Yes," Gene answered.

It was the first time he'd ever paid a man for sex. It was worth every penny of what he paid for it, he thought.

Tray was a bull, as Gene had assumed he would be. They lay on the bed in Manny's apartment, Tray stretched out on top of Gene, and they kissed and fondled each other and ran their hands over each other's bodies in a mutual total exploration of the other. Tray, in full exhilarating erection, was able to hold himself in check until the heat of Gene's need built up to the point of sobbing and begging for the cock. Even then, Gene had to take the cock in hand, Tray lying between his spread legs, guide it to his hole, and raise his pelvis to it.

Tray's thrust was slow and deep. Gene groaned deeply, raised his arms over his head to grasp the top rung of the headboard, and arched his back. He moaned and panted as Tray slow pumped him up the scale of arousal and need into the clouds of ecstasy. While Tray was fucking him, he was reciting poetry—a poem with a heavy beat that matched the timing of his thrusts, his cock bottoming out at the rhyming ends of lines. Gene hadn't been moved like this during sex since Josh Steinem had fucked him before Gene had gone to Kenton Blackburn's bed in Chicago. It was only now that Gene realized that this was the quality of sex that he ached for.

The next day he remained in the apartment, writing feverishly, trying to ensure that he captured all of the passion that the black poet had fucked into him before it evaporated.

And that evening, exhausted, he thought. He thought of Tray, the fucking poet, but as he sat and thought, the image of Josh Steinem slowly intruded into his mind to take over his musings.

So, on Tuesday afternoon, he was standing in front of the five-story brownstone on 39th Street and watching Josh Steinem through the display window of the menswear shop pinning together pieces of a tuxedo on a worktable as shop assistants and a tailor bustled around him seeing to the needs of a few male customers.

As he looked he noticed a "help wanted" sign in the window and, soon after that, Josh looked up and out of the window, saw Gene standing there, and smiled. It was as if it had just been yesterday that they had last met—and maybe, Gene fancifully thought, just maybe it had been as recently as Saturday. Just maybe the spirit of Josh had been inside the body of the black bull poet, Tray.

Gene entered the shop, turned and took the "help wanted" sign out of the window, and then turned again and walked over to where Josh was perched on a stool behind the worktable.

"You have a job opening here?"

"Not for you," Josh said.

Gene hesitated. He hadn't thought of the possibility of rejection. That scenario hadn't entered his mind. He was on the edge of crushed.

But Josh saved him. "The opening is for a custodian. If you come to work here, you'll have to work as a model and you'll have to work on the literary journal that publishes upstairs. And you'll have even more challenging work upstairs in my apartment. It will be exhausting work."

"It sound like exactly what I'm looking for," Gene said.

"You'd have to live in. The job would use you full time, 24/7."

"The job's beginning to sound even better," Gene said.

"There will be an audition. I know you've auditioned before, but I would want to be refreshed about your skills . . . your considerable skills, if I recall rightly."

"Should I make an appointment?"

"You can go upstairs and wait for me. I have a bit more to do here. I think you can find your way."

And Gene did find his way.

Later that afternoon, he lay, exhausted, on his belly, on Josh's bed, his arm dangling over the side of the bed and his eyes watching Josh, standing naked in the doorway to his bathroom and drying off after his shower. They had fucked twice and Josh had taken his time doing it.

Gene's thoughts went to what he wanted in a man. He couldn't think why Josh didn't have it all. Could he think of this as "it"? Of course he could, if for no other reason than that this wasn't an easy Sunday. This was Tuesday. And he'd been taken to the top, repeatedly, and over the top twice.

His cellphone went off. He reached over, took it off the nightstand, looked at the text message, and laughed. Then he tapped in an answer, put the cellphone back on the nightstand, and reclined back into the pillows on the bed.

"Something amusing?" Josh asked.

"My California agent sold the movie rights to my first novel at last—he took it to another studio from the one we were trying, without much success. He wants me to come out to L.A. to sign the contracts."

"So, you off for California again?" Josh asked. He couldn't keep the disappointment out of his voice.

"Not on your life. I'm just starting a dream job here. I told him to find an agent to handle my end of the signing here in New York or to forget it. That's if, of course, I passed the job audition here. Did I?"

"What do you think?"

"Well, it sure went well for me. What about for you?"

"I can't be sure. I think the audition should continue. Of course, it will mean I've got to take another shower because I'm going to be getting all hot and bothered again."

Both men were smiling as Josh walked back to the bed, walking carefully to avoid the two spent condoms he'd tossed on the floor, while fully determined to add to that collection.

About the Author

Habu is one of the pen names of a former supersonic spy jet pilot, intelligence agent, male model, movie actor, and diplomat. A wild youth in Southeast Asia was spent enjoying whatever sexual opportunities came his way, and much of his gay male writing is about recalling incidents from those days and inventing ones he'd perhaps have liked to experience. He now leads a very quiet and ordinary happily married family life.

An American, he is a published mainstream novelist and short story writer under another name and in another dimension of his life. He has written or cowritten (with Sabb) approaching 1,000 published short stories and over 100 published erotica e-books, primarily of gay fiction but also memoir, straight fiction and ménage fiction. His hand and creative writing can be seen in stories and books by habu, sr71plt, Dirk Hessian, Shabbu, and Stephen Kessel— among unrevealed others that might surprise readers. The fictionalized GM memoir *Flying High, Diving Deep* is loosely based on his life experiences. He can be found at the adults only gay male site BarbarianSpy, which he shares with Sabb and Dirk Hessian.

Our authors always like to receive feedback, and appreciate it when readers post reviews at distributors and other sites.

BarbarianSpy Books

Not all books listed below may currently be on release.
* indicates the book is available in paperback and e-book.

BOOKS BY CHRIS CROSS
Multisexual Adult Romance

Pulaski Square
Chocolate in Vanilla (MF)2
Christmas with Chris (MMF) (MM) (MF)

BOOKS BY ALEX LOCKHEED
Transgender Romance

Meeting Jenna

Transgender Other

Being Sarah

BOOKS BY DIRK HESSIAN
Xtreme Historical Erotica

Dirk's Ancient Times Collection (Print only Bundle)*
The King's Men
Shores of Tripoli*
Prophecy of Noto
Pretender's Fate

General Historical Erotic Romance

Dirk's America's Founding Collection (Print only Bundle)*
Soldier,Spy
Ridden West
Deliver a Virgin
Clouds and Rain
Confederate Gold
Puttin on the Ritz
To the Hessian Hills
Fire Down the Valley*
Constantinople*
The Beautiful Way*
Blue and Gray
Colonel's Treasure
Beginning of Time
Labyrinth
Big Sky Country

BOOKS BY HABU

Gay Erotica
Memoir Faction
Flying High, Diving Deep*
Xtreme Erotica
Fist of Gold
Liaisons
Chain Gang Banged (Short Story)
Tramp Steaming*
Escape to Girne
Silas' Choice*
Last Call
Choke Hold
Apyko: The Greek Pimp
Visits of the Schlange
Second Coming: Emile La Cour Unleashed*
Vortex: Sacrificed by Curiosity*
Dark Angel Sounding *(in e-book & included in Sounding:Ultimate Control paperback)**
Sounding: Ultimate Control (*Print Only*)*
Sounding Five *(in e-book & included in Sounding:Ultimate Control paperback)**
Romance
Gift from the Sea
Shore Leave
The Aviators
Poison Pen
Need to be Needed
Key Westing (short)
Finding a New Sam
Bangkok Summer Seduction
The Photograph
Inevitable Case
Turn to Love
Rain Check
Built for Pleasure (Sci Fi)
Danny's Choice*
Pull of the Groove
Sugar n Spice Christmas
Friday Nights with Lenny (Christmas Romance)
Snowy, Snowy Nights (Christmas Romance)
Tank n Bull
Sail to the Sun
War Letters
Ravens Roost
Caribbean Cruise Top to Bottom
Arena Stage

Trading Partners (Valentine's Day)
Four Coins
Lower Than the Heart (Valentine's Day)
Brambleton
Finding Amnad
Platres Conclave
Different Strokes
Other Novels/Novellas
Also Want to Thank
Ranger Guided
Key Westing
Syrian Ram
Temptation's Clutches*
Descent into Chaos
Escape to Girne
Journey Through Abilene
Harmony and Dissonance
Stallion Station
Racing With the Devil (espionage suspense)
Prepared in Cape Verdi
Gilded Cage
House on Park*
Anything for Ambition
Dance of the Ravishers
Hard Knocks U*
My Neighbor's Spa*
Man's Man: Tales of a High Priced Gay Hooker*
Trip Money
The Indian Doctor
Sailorboy
Home to Fire Island
Switching Sides*
Murder Mysteries
Retribution (Hardesty)
Snitches (Hardesty
Gotta Keep Trying (Hardesty)
All Fools Day Foolery (Mike Kavanagh)
Inevitable Case (Mike Kavanagh)
Vanishing Laura
Death on a Ping Pong Table
Clint Folsom Mysteries Compendium Volume 1*
Death to Blonds - Stolen Judgment (Clint Folsom Mystery)*
Clint Folsom Mysteries Compendium Volume 2*

Gay Erotica Anthologies

A Hell of a War*
Earth Cry*
Shunga
Habu's Christmas Balls
Eight in D*
DevilMENt
Silas' Choices*
Stallion Station (A Novella in Parts)
Eleven to the Dogs*
Fifty Seventy*
Spy Tails 001*
Spy Tails 002*
Doubled*
Doubled Again*
Tails in the Tropics*
Tails in the Med*
Tails in the West*
Rough Riders*
Grab Bag 1*
Grab Bag 2*
Grab Bag 3*
Grab Bag 4*
Grab Bag 5*
Grab Bag 6*
Grab Bag 7*
Grab Bag 8*
Grab Bag 9*
Grab Bag 10*
Grab Bag 11*
Grab Bag 12*
Grab Bag 13*
Grab Bag 14*
Beyond the Beaded Curtain*
On the Train
The Sporting Life*
Fetish Galore!*
Literary Gay Erotica
Cairo Surrender*
The Handyman*
Homeward Bound
Journey to Mirage*
Bisexual/Menage/Multisexual Erotica
And Eat it Too
Two Men, One Woman*
Every Which Way
Summer of Denial

Death on a Ping Pong Table
Cruising Gigolo
13 Ways for Halloween
Luther*
The Indian Prince*
BOOKS BY SABB
Spanish Lovers
Driver Reliever
Hiring in Hollywood
The Legend of Holleystone Grange
Surprise Encounters*
She is He
Wrong Man
Loyal to his King
Barbarian Tales - Book One - Traveler's Tales*
Barbarian Tales - Book Two - Journeys Begin*
Barbarian Tales - Book Three - The Inheritance*
Barbarian Tales - Book Four - Road to Persepolis*
BOOKS BY SHABBU
A Season in Galicia*
Blind Dates*
Velvet Interrogation
Finding Jason
Dirty Pool
Operation Black Jade
Cigars!*
Angel in the Barn
Gayly Complicated*
Despoiling David
The Tree of Idleness*
I Met a Man
Rough Road to Happiness
BOOKS BY STEPHEN KESSEL
Gay Romance
The Forever Man
Two Chances
BOOKS BY KIM BLACK
Lesbian Romance
Transfixed on Tammie (F/T lesbian)

*****